All These Little Worlds

All These Little Worlds
The Fiction Desk Anthology Series
Volume Two

Edited by Rob Redman

The Fiction Desk

First published in the UK in 2011 by The Fiction Desk Ltd.

ISBN 978-0-9567843-2-2

The Fiction Desk
PO Box 116
Rye
TN31 9DY

Please note that we do not accept postal submissions.
See our website for submissions information.

www.thefictiondesk.com

The Fiction Desk Ltd
Registered in the UK, no 07410083
Registered office: 3rd Floor, 207 Regent Street, London, W1B 3HH

Printed and bound in the UK by Imprint Digital.

Contents

Introduction   7
Rob Redman

Jaggers & Crown   11
James Benmore

Swimming with the Fishes   35
Jennifer Moore

Pretty Vacant   43
Charles Lambert

Room 307   75
Mischa Hiller

Contents

Dress Code   93
  Halimah Marcus

The Romantic   117
  Colin Corrigan

After All the Fun We Had   125
  Ryan Shoemaker

"Glenda"   137
  Andrew Jury

Get on Green   151
  Jason Atkinson

About the Contributors   165

Introduction

Rob Redman

The Fiction Desk anthologies aren't themed.

It's sometimes tempting to publish a themed volume, to put together *The Germany Edition* or *Forty Stories About Rabbits* or *New Voices from Peckham*. Themed anthologies would be much easier to sell, and the covers would virtually design themselves—assuming you could get forty rabbits to sit still for a photo shoot.

The problem with themed anthologies is that they would represent a missed opportunity, or a whole series of missed opportunities. Part of it comes down to the way stories reach us: we have an open submissions policy for our anthology series, and for every story that we accept, we see maybe another hundred. Sometimes it's more, sometimes a little less. Of those hundred stories, some aren't quite good enough, or aren't quite right for us, or are too long or too short or too much like another story we've already accepted.

If we spent three months only accepting submissions centred on a specific theme, not only would we have to turn down all the stories that aren't quite right for us or good enough, but we'd also have to turn down all the stories that weren't Germanic, or rabbity, or Peckhamy enough.

The other argument against themed anthologies is down to the reading experience: such a tight collection might feel like a novelty at first, but with a whole universe out there, and thousands of years of recorded human experience, does anybody *really* want to only read stories about fruit?

(Perhaps some people do; and they will have to make do with the reference to a tomato that appears on page 98 of this volume.)

Still, despite all attempts to keep the stories varied, connected only in terms of the standard of the writing, more specific themes do crop up. There's a definite synchronicity to the submissions pile: one day, every story that arrives will feature a baked Alaska; another, we'll get three stories in a row, from different parts of the world, in which somebody has to replace a dead goldfish before the owner discovers their loss. I try to filter these patterns out as part of the submissions process, to keep a sense of variety in the published stories, but sometimes they creep through.

In *All These Little Worlds*, you'll find three separate stories about the education system in America: 'Dress Code' gives us the experiences of a new teacher at an exclusive private school, 'After All the Fun We Had' recounts the experiences of an embittered principal, and 'Get on Green' shows us a school day through the eyes of a young pupil. The settings, stories, and voices of the narrators are diverse enough that I completely failed to notice the connection when I was selecting the stories, and if I'd realised by the time it came to designing the cover, with its use of blackboard chalk, the realisation was only subconscious.

When I did finally see what had happened, I kicked myself and considered splitting the stories over two volumes to break up the pattern, but in the end I decided it works rather well. There's something satisfying about a volume that has a hint of a theme, just enough to give the collection a character of its own, but without boxing the stories in.

So this isn't *Nine Stories About Education*, unless you hold it up to the light in a certain way and squint. The title instead is a more universal one, and refers to that particular alchemy you find in good short stories, through which they create entire worlds with just a handful of words, worlds that seem to stretch much further and contain far more than the little piece that's visible through the window that the story opens on to them.

*In 'Jaggers & Crown', the narrator's voice is so convincing
that I think I believe in Kevin Crown more than I do in James
Benmore. But James assures me he's real, and adds that he's
currently at work on a novel about the Artful Dodger.*

Jaggers & Crown

James Benmore

According to this morning's paper, I am meant to have died
sometime over the weekend. Go and buy a copy of *The Mail* if you
don't believe me; I'm on page 36.

Now you imagine coming across such a odd thing yourself. You
get out of bed, bright and early, thinking it's just another morning.
You wash, get dressed and take the dog out for his morning walk,
if you have a dog that is. On the way back you stop off at the corner
shop, as you often do, to buy yourself a paper and a few other bits
and then you're off to your favourite café to read it over breakfast.
You're halfway through your bacon and eggs and there, on page
36, is you. An old black and white photograph of you and the
words underneath are telling you how sadly missed you now are.
Well, if you're anything like me I think you'd be quite unsettled
by the experience.

'Maisie,' I called over. 'Here, Maisie. Take a look at this.'
Maisie was behind the counter and looked busy so I shouldn't

have pestered her. But I felt overcome by this sudden need to talk to someone.

'Give us a minute, Kev,' she called back. Sat at a table opposite mine was this old gentleman, about my age, and he was using this opportunity to get my attention. He comes here a lot, I think I'm half the reason, and on this occasion he smiled over and said, 'Nice One, You Nit!' Normally I'm quite responsive to my old catchphrases but on this occasion I wasn't in the mood.

'Maisie,' I continued, ignoring him. 'My spectacles must be playing up. Read this for me.'

'What's up, Kev?' she said as she scuttled across. 'It's not Jingo, is it? He hasn't disgraced himself again?'

'No, love,' I assured her, stroking Jingo on the head. He was in his usual spot under the table chewing on some bacon fat but, considering his previous mishaps, she was right to be wary. 'He's as good as gold. It's this.' I pointed to the publicity shot that the paper had seen fit to mark my passing with. I was dressed up as a garden gnome, with the pointy hat and fishing rod in my hands, and it must have been taken over forty years ago.

'Goodness, Kevin, I've not seen this one before. I'll tell you what, we'll cut it out and stick it up with the others.' Maisie, you see, is one of our biggest admirers. Up at the counter, for everyone to see, she has created a super collage out of clippings of Sonny and myself that she has collected over the years. There's that iconic image of Sonny pretending to strangle me while I mug to the camera, as well as various stills of us performing our most famous scenes. All of these are dotted around an original poster for our live show, A *Night on the Town with Jaggers & Crown*, which I have been happy to sign for her. But, lovely woman though she is, she was missing the point.

'Look what page it's on, Maisie. The obituary page. This is my own obituary I'm sat here looking at.' I prodded the words at the bottom of the page.

KEVIN CROWN 1930-2011

'Your obituary?' she laughed. 'You're not dead, are you?' She scanned the page and read the first paragraph.

> 'Little' Kevin Crown, one half of the once popular double act Jaggers & Crown, has died aged 81. He and his comedy partner Sonny Jaggers enjoyed huge fame on both radio and television before their success was brought to an untimely end by the sudden death of Jaggers in 1966.

'How funny!' she said. I told her I didn't see what was so very amusing about it, and this is when the old gentleman decided to stick his oar in.

'Perhaps they've printed yours instead of someone else's,' he suggested. 'Pulled the wrong one out of the file. I'm told these papers have obituaries already written out for those they think'll die soon.' He said that with a grin.

'In that case, they must've had Kevin's on standby for years,' laughed Maisie. I gave the old boy one of my looks to let him know that I hadn't asked for his tuppence and he soon went back to his sausages. 'This is like something from one of your old shows, Kev,' Maisie continued. 'What was that one where the two of you ran that funeral parlour and you almost ended up burying Sonny by accident?' She was referring to 'Good Grief', one of the better episodes from series two. 'Well, this obituary business reminds me of that.'

And even though I did feel quite rattled by this occurrence, I knew what she meant. I could imagine an episode of *No Need to Frown* beginning with either myself or Sonny reading our own obituary one morning. The rest of the show would have been about us trying to get the paper to print a public apology, which is maybe what I should have been doing. But instead I just found myself looking down at the page and noticing how little space they had devoted to me. When Sonny died he had made the front page of most of the papers. I suppose that was only natural though, considering how young he was.

> Born in South London, Kevin Crown was the only son of Violet and Arthur Crown, both of whom were music hall ventriloquists. As a child he became a performer himself. He was a natural comedian but only achieved modest success as a solo act. Fortunately, his luck turned in 1952 when destiny intervened.

The first time I ever met Sonny, face to face, was in a hotel tea room in Portsmouth. I was coming to the end of my military service and was stationed in barracks and myself and a few of the lads had been to the Portsmouth Playhouse the night before and had seen him in his touring show. *The Sonny Jaggers Revue* had completely bowled me over; it was the sort of risky comedy that I wanted to be doing myself. Sonny had written most of it himself and the sketches were full of the type of dodgy innuendo that I daresay wouldn't impress someone of the current generation, what with all the filth they watch, but this was the early fifties and he's lucky the police weren't called. There was all this business about the queer behaviour of the rear-gunner and about cleaning up the officer's mess. That sort of thing.

Now the lad who played all the other parts in the show was the actor Clive Woad. As it happened, I knew Clive quite well because some years prior we had performed together in panto, playing two halves of the same horse. And so the next morning I contacted Clive to ask him if he could introduce me to Sonny. Why, he wanted to know. I said you know why, Clive, to help forward my career. Clive said 'I see,' before phoning back a few hours later to say that Sonny would be happy to meet me that afternoon at his hotel. Sonny likes the sound of you, he said.

The tea room in the Queen's Hotel was a spotless, formal sort of place that would have appealed to Sonny's delicate sensibilities. It was an airy conservatory that overlooked the sea and they insisted on a strict dress code, even though they were only serving tea and scones. I've always been a presentable fellow however, and I arrived with my shoes shined and suit pressed. I had made such an effort for this meeting that, as I was getting ready to leave the barracks, the lad who slept in the bunk beside me commented that I must be off to see some new girl. I didn't correct him; he wouldn't have understood.

A waitress approached me as I entered and I told her that I had come to take tea with a Mr Jaggers who was a guest at this hotel. She raised her eyebrow and said 'I see' in much the same manner that Clive had said 'I see' on the phone earlier. I don't know what she thought she was insinuating, she looked about fourteen. The place was almost empty and the girl pointed towards a table where a man was sat alone reading a newspaper. I didn't recognise him at first, he seemed older and posher than he did onstage. He was dressed flamboyantly, as theatricals often are, but his lavender shirt and cravat made him look a lot a lot more moneyed than anybody I knew in show business. As I approached his table I felt myself becoming littler.

'Mr Jaggers,' I said. 'My name's Kevin Crown. I'm a friend of Clive's.' He looked up from his paper and smiled.

'I could smell you coming, you know,' he said, surveying me from top to toe. 'There was a strong waft of Brylcreem that entered the room moments before you did. No, don't apologise, I rather like it. I admire anyone who'll apply the stuff with scant regard for fashionable tastes.' He rose from his seat and saluted. 'You must be the army boy,' he said grinning. 'I had hoped you would be in uniform but it doesn't matter, I'm not disappointed. Have a seat.'

All this struck me as an affectation. I knew for a fact that his Dad had worked in a factory. 'Clive always knows the friendliest people,' he continued, 'which is surprising considering what a graceless brute he can be. I hope you enjoy afternoon tea. I've ordered us scones and cucumber sandwiches. I'll be mother.' As he picked up the teapot and began pouring through the strainer, I noticed his nice watch and the unusual fragrance he was wearing. I wanted to ask him how much he was earning but it was too early for that.

'I saw your show last night, Mr Jaggers,' I said instead, 'and I thought it was tremendous.'

'How sweet of you to say, Colin. I can see that you and I will be getting along famously.' He leaned over and patted my knee just as the waitress arrived with the sandwiches and scones and another look. I found myself shifting away from him. If Sonny noticed he didn't show it and we sat awkwardly for a bit while he buttered my scones and said how the strawberry jam here was the best in England. I said very little. Sonny then began telling me how important he felt military service was to a growing lad such as myself and about how I made him proud to be British.

'I'm an aspiring comedian myself actually,' I blurted out suddenly when he paused to eat a sandwich. 'I imagine Clive mentioned it.'

'No, he didn't,' Sonny said flatly.

'Oh yeah, I've had plenty of experience in pantomime and all that. And I was the star performer in the variety shows that the army put on. I'm what you might call a voice man. I can do all different classes, accents, foreigners, women. And I can impersonate whoever you want. You name a famous person and I'll do 'em. Go on.' Sonny's body stiffened. I could tell he thought I'd hit the first bum note of the afternoon.

'Please,' he said in a heavier tone than before, 'I'll take your word for it.'

'I do all the big stars,' I continued regardless. 'I'll do you if you like.' And before he could stop me I was impersonating his voice. Not his real voice, but his performance voice with all those strangulated vowels and effeminate, high-pitched inflections. I don't know why but I thought he'd enjoy it. Instead, he rolled his newspaper up, and hit me over the head with it.

'That's enough of that,' he said. 'I don't wish to listen to you showing off all afternoon. I wish to enjoy my tea.' He sat back, as if in a sulk, and continued sipping at his cup.

'I'm ever so sorry, Mr Jaggers,' I said, rubbing my head like Stan Laurel. 'I didn't mean to offend. I just wanted to show you what I can do. Thing is,' I continued as he drank, 'I think, if you gave me a chance, I could be a great asset to your show.' Sonny almost snorted some liquid out of his nostrils.

'Oh, behave yourself,' he said. 'My show doesn't need your help.'

I'm not proud of what I said next. I was grateful to my old mate Clive for putting me in touch with Sonny but I felt compelled to speak honestly. 'Well, as I say, I enjoyed your show very much. I think you're an amazing talent, honestly I do.' Sonny nodded casually. 'But, and this may seem a bit disloyal of me, I don't think you're being well served by your straight man. Not in my opinion.'

'Mr Woad?'

'Yeah, Clive,' I said. 'Don't get me wrong, I love him to bits. But he's not a natural performer. I worked with him in panto once and he couldn't even play a horse's arse properly.'

Sonny chuckled. He admired a bit of cheek and I could feel him softening again. 'Clive is very ordinary,' he agreed. 'But why should I care? After all, we're not a double act. He's just the stooge.'

'Well, that is where you're making a mistake, if you'll forgive my bluntness. The way things are now, Clive is undermining your show when he should be contributing to it. You should never underestimate the importance of a first-class straight man. You could double your laughs if you had someone a bit more responsive, with sharper timing. And a good reaction character helps the audience know how they should be taking some of your more awkward material.'

'Awkward material?' he said, employing the familiar eyebrow arch that he overused in his later performances.

'The suspect parts,' I said lowering my voice so that the waitress wouldn't hear. 'The parts that refer to, you know, homosexuals.' Sonny's reaction was loud enough for the whole tea room.

'What a bloomin' slur!' he shrieked, pretending to be scandalised. 'There's nothing suspect about my act, dear. It's your own dirty little mind making up your own jokes!' I begged him to shush. It was alright for Sonny to play the outraged queen, but I still had to live in this town.

'A larger audience,' I continued, once he'd finished grand-standing. 'Families. The sort of audience that listens to the wireless. Well, your act might make them uncomfortable. But if you had someone for that audience in your show, a straight man if you like, then that would help. It would give you the common touch.' I paused for a moment and shrugged. 'But what do I know? You're probably not interested in a larger audience.'

Sonny drained the remains of his tea. Then he became unnaturally still and just stared into his cup. 'And you think that you can provide that, do you?' he said at last. 'The common touch.'

'Probably, yeah. You'd still be the funny one, though. It's your show, after all.'

Sonny continued to inspect the bottom of his cup. When he spoke again he sounded odd, as though he had only just noticed me. 'What did you say your name was?' he asked.

'Kevin Crown.'

'And do you believe in clairvoyance, Kevin Crown?'

'You mean, fortune-telling and that?'

'Yes,' he said. 'Palm readings, tea-leaves and the like.' He looked at me now with an absent expression. 'Because I do. I'm a great believer in the world beyond this.' He swirled his cup about. 'There is a woman I sometimes go to visit in Tooting who calls herself Madame Hilda. She's terribly good. I visited her a fortnight ago and guess what? She mentioned you.'

'Did she?' I said. I didn't like talking about mediums, they unnerved me. I was going to joke that I preferred a large but I imagine he'd probably heard that one.

'She said that a new friend would reveal himself. One with a large, yet perfidious heart.' I wasn't sure how to take that. I didn't even know what perfidious meant.

Sonny seemed to snap out of it then. He glanced at his watch. 'I've got a bottle of whisky in my room, Kevin, and a performance in three hours. I'll tell you what, let's go upstairs for a tipple and you can help me with my lines. And then perhaps you can show me this common touch of yours.' He jumped to his feet and indicated to the waitress that we were finished. 'And by the way,' he said, 'Mr Jaggers is my father. Call me Sonny.'

> Sonny Jaggers had taken an instant liking to his diminutive admirer and when Kevin was discharged from the army he joined Sonny on his nationwide tour as his personal dresser. Soon after, Clive Woad left the show due to creative differences and the plucky Kevin proved to be a more than capable replacement. From that day on, Jaggers never performed without Crown and when the BBC commissioned a new radio series called *Jaggers & Friends*, Kevin proved to be a key part of the show's success.

That radio show was where I came into my own. In each programme Sonny played Sonny, and I played everyone else. My comic turns were considered to be the high point for many listeners and I created a number of memorable characters such as Haggis McSkinty, Old Widow Crabs and, of course, Poppadom Patel. Sadly, I had to scrap a lot of this material when the corporation suddenly issued something called the ' Blue Book' to all its performers. This contained a set of guidelines that seemed designed to stifle our creativity. I remember going over the rules with Sonny on the day of a recording.

'Programmes must kept free of crudities, coarseness and innuendo,' I read aloud.

'Marvellous,' he said. 'That's our whole act.' We were in his flat waiting for a taxi to collect us but he was still in his dressing gown, lounging on the settee. On the side table was a bottle of brandy and every few minutes he would pour and drink another glass. I had long since given up trying to persuade him not to booze before shows.

'There is to be an absolute ban on jokes concerning lavatories, gentlemen meeting in lavatories, effeminacy in men, prostitution, ladies' underwear, marital infidelity, physical infirmities, mental infirmities, animals' habits (e.g. rabbits), biblical parodies, the sayings of Christ and descriptions of Him, offensive references to Jews (or any other religious sect), derogatory references to the working classes, foreign stereotypes and jokes about drunkenness.'

'Well,' Sonny yawned, standing to stretch himself, glass still in hand, 'they've given us plenty to work with.' He downed the last of the brandy and headed to the wardrobe to look for a suit.

'Trade slogans are barred and any impersonations will require the permission of the person being impersonated prior to performance. Do not refer to *niggers*, *coons*, *sambos*, or *negroes*. If necessary, the safest term is *coloured*, although the corporation would prefer it if you omitted all reference to race in a light entertainment broadcast. Expletives have no place in light entertainment and such words as *damn*, *blast*, *hell*, *bloody*, *gorblimey* and *ruddy* should be deleted from scripts with immediate effect.'

'How about *fuck*?' said Sonny as he buttoned his shirt. 'Does it mention that anywhere?' I told him that no, it didn't. 'Good,' he said, as I knotted his tie for him. 'Then I shall look forward to saying it regularly.'

But no matter how drunk he was, Sonny was always an impeccable performer. At least he was whenever he showed up. What my obituary doesn't mention is the occasion when Sonny went missing for a week and I had to rescue things using my own talents. This would have been in 1959, towards the end of our radio run, and Sonny and I had begun to grow apart, socially speaking. We still had a decent working relationship but he had begun associating with his new Soho set, all playwrights and serious actors, not my type of people at all. And these so-called friends had brought out the worst in him, in my view. He was forever getting himself into relationships with people that only cared about his money, and his drinking worsened with every heartbreak. Anyway, that was none of my business, I wasn't interested in how he conducted himself in his spare time, but it was starting to affect work. Very often he arrived late to a recording, not having learnt his own scripts, and in these foul moods. And then, on this particular day, he didn't arrive at all.

By this time we were being represented by Chas Wimold, of Wimold Artistes, a gruff northerner who had surprisingly little patience for the artistic temperament considering the line of work he was in. When he heard that Sonny had disappeared he came down to the theatre where our shows were recorded to throw a fit.

'I've been hearing about a very exciting film project,' he announced as he stomped about backstage. 'It's called *The Vanishing Poof*, and your pal is perfect for the lead.' I tried to assure him that there was nothing to worry about, that Sonny was sure to appear at any moment, but Chas was unconvinced. 'I've spent three ruddy months trying to convince the BBC to move your show to the telly. And just when it looks like they're about to commission us, this happens. Well, if he misses this performance you can kiss goodbye to *Jaggers & Crown*.'

'Jaggers and what?'

'*Jaggers & Crown*. That's what I was going to insist the two of you are to be billed as from now on. The television show was to be called *No Need to Frown, it's Jaggers & Crown*.'

'Are you sure, Charlie? I can imagine what Sonny will say.'

'Who cares what that jumped-up fairy thinks?' he said. 'It's been plain to me for some time that you're the one the public like best. You've got the common touch.' Well, he said it, not me. 'Still,' Chas continued, 'it's academic now. They won't let you on the box if we have to go out there and tell the audience to clear out because Jaggers is dead in a ditch somewhere.'

The recording had already been postponed for just under an hour. Sonny clearly wasn't coming and Chas had resigned himself to the fact that we were finished in broadcasting.

'Hang about, Charlie,' I said, just as the producers were about to apologise to the audience and cancel the recording, 'I've had an idea.'

Most of our radio programmes were performed in front of a crowd of less than two hundred people and many of these punters had now shuffled off home. The announcer, a fellow called Nigel, went onstage and informed the remaining crowd that unfortunately Sonny Jaggers would not be performing today because of a throat infection. But, if they were prepared to remain seated, the show would go on with the role of Sonny Jaggers now being played by Kevin Crown.

'Are you sure you can manage all this, Kevin?' asked Nigel, moments before the trombonist struck up the *Jaggers & Friends* theme tune. The script involved Sonny deciding he was going to join the circus as a juggler but, after making some snide remarks about the bearded lady, he is tricked into walking the tightrope, taming a lion and having to motorcycle his way through a flaming hoop, all by her enraged dwarf husband. I already had to play the roles of the lady, the dwarf, the ringmaster, two French clowns and the bloke who clears away the elephant mess, so one more character wouldn't hurt. 'Make sure you pause for breath,' Nigel warned.

'Don't fret, Nigel,' I said, 'I know what I'm doing.' I had the script propped up on a music stand in front of the microphones with all my bits underlined in blue ink and Sonny's in red. Earlier that morning I had been rehearsing the script aloud and, with Sonny absent, I'd been delivering his lines myself anyway. So, with the audience in on our little secret, the recording began with Nigel declaring that it was another episode of 'Jaggers & Friends, starring Sonny Jaggers' and we were back in business.

The whole thing went off without a hitch. Sonny had a distinctive performing style, but not only could I mimic that peculiar nasal drone of his, I had also studied his timing. Throughout the show I took great care to hold a silence for three, four, even five seconds, a Sonny Jaggers pause. Afterwards, Nigel told me that I had proved myself to be a better Jaggers than Jaggers, and Chas said that if it were up to him the TV programme would be called *Crown & Friends*. The audience had been lovely and I received twice the laughs that we would have done otherwise and a thunderous round of applause at the end. The listeners at home, for whom it was just another show, must have wondered what the fuss was about.

When the show was broadcast days later, Sonny was still missing. I had wanted to notify the police but Chas talked me out of it, saying that if we made a fuss the press would smell blood and want to know about Sonny's private life. Sonny would pop up, he assured me, when the money ran out. The next night Sonny reappeared, he knocked on my front door with a dismal expression on his face and asked me to forgive his awful behaviour. I let him in and he stayed the night.

He explained that he had been led astray by the famous actor Sir George Shatillion, and the two of them had gone on an almighty bender and just about buggered every rent-boy in the capital. Sonny had been under the impression he had found love with Sir George, but had been cruelly rejected when the actor announced that he had no intention of leaving Mrs Shatillion. Sonny had been in a very black place since then and began sobbing to me about his unshared life, about being alone. I reminded him that he wasn't alone. He had me.

'I hardly recall a thing, y'know,' he said the next morning over breakfast. 'I don't remember where we drank, where we slept, who I met. Do you know, I can't even remember recording that programme last Monday. I was bloody amazed to hear myself on the wireless yesterday.' He smiled and drank his coffee. 'It's nice to know I'm still funny.'

> The *Jaggers & Crown* TV show was first broadcast in 1960 and was an instant hit. Their double-act was now firmly established with Crown playing the regular role of Little Kevin. The premise was that they were struggling comedians living in squalor, and each week Sonny would try to break free from this rut by finding a new vocation, only to have his attempts ruined by the well-meaning yet idiotic Kevin. The show ran for six years and Sonny's catchphrases, 'Behave yourself', 'Nice one, you Nit', and 'I'm in the Pink' delighted viewers throughout the land.

Whenever I read about how much these modern celebrities are getting paid by the BBC it makes me want to spit on my TV license. Back when Jaggers and Crown were the corporation's star performers, we were on a fraction of what comedians were earning on Independent Television. Ken Knott, for example, used to drive around in a silver Bentley with KNOTT 1 on the registration plate, and Humphrey Pickle had a second home in Marbella. But you never met anyone who admitted to watching ITV's rip-off show *Giggle a Lot, it's Pickle and Knott*, so we were clearly undervalued. Then, at the end of our fifth series, ITV offered us four times the amount if we defected to them. Our current black-and-white show was being shot on videotape and transmitted live so you could see the cheap sets wobble and hear every drunken slur in Sonny's words. But the proposed new series was to be filmed in full colour at Elstree studios, with plenty of exterior scenes and enough takes for Sonny to get it right. This extra polish meant that the series could be sold to the American networks, so I was naturally keen to switch. However, some alterations were required and Chas Wimold arranged a meeting in his Soho office to discuss them.

'You need to make the show less queer,' he told myself and Archie Dunn. Archie was a scriptwriter, the man responsible for creating Little Kevin, and he was producing most of our material now that Sonny could only manage three hundred words a week. Sonny had been summoned to Chas's pow-wow too but, as was typical, he hadn't appeared. He seemed to have lost interest in the business side of things and he'd begun to hold Chas in contempt. Sonny used to say that there was nothing more odious than having to watch a fat man smoke a cigar.

'All that sexual innuendo that Jaggers likes,' Chas continued, lighting up a Havana, 'ITV doesn't. "I'm in the Pink!" That business about you two sharing a bed. Finish it.' He was referring to the end of every show where myself and Sonny discuss the day's events in a brass bed before we turned out the lights.

'I don't see that part of the show as queer, Chas,' said Archie, who had a wife and kids and had come up with the idea. 'Laurel and Hardy were often filmed in the same bed. The idea is to show that they live in such impoverished conditions that they sleep together for warmth. It's supposed to be funny, not suggestive.'

'Sonny and I are very careful to keep our hands where people can see them,' I added. 'He's always reading a book and I'm forever wiping my spectacles, so the viewer is comfortable that there's nothing going on underneath the covers.' But Chas was unconvinced.

'When Laurel and Hardy shared a bed it was funny because it was ridiculous,' he argued. 'Nobody thought they were poofs because they didn't seem like poofs. That doesn't apply to Jaggers and Crown.'

I was confused by this remark because over the years I'd been cultivating the image of a ladies' man. A number of photographs of myself strolling arm-in-arm with various dolly birds had been circulated in the national press, and Archie had written several plots into the series where Little Kevin has his heart broken by girls. Archie broke the awkward silence.

'Sonny is rather camp,' he said. 'But that's what makes him Sonny. The viewers love him for it.'

'Well, the advertisers don't. If you've got any sense you'll tell ITV that you intend to tone him down. He can still be effeminate, that's very funny, but stop making suggestions that he enjoys it so much.'

'Maybe in the new series he should be sadder, more sexless,' Archie suggested. 'He could live with his mum instead of Kevin and the scripts could make fun of him more.' Chas asked for an example. 'Well, Sonny could say something like "What do I have to do to be a good man?" and Kevin could zing him back with "you have to be a man for a start, you bloomin' great shirt-lifter." The three of us roared at that.

'That's good,' I said. 'It assures the audience that, while Sonny might be a fairy, I'm definitely not.' Chas produced two of his fattest cigars for us, opened a bottle of brandy and we talked some more about the show's new direction.

About a month before this, Sonny had been admitted to a London nursing home to be treated for, as the press were told, nervous exhaustion. I'd been to visit him there and we'd had a blazing row in which he said some very hurtful things about my performance style. He said that Little Kevin had even fewer dimensions than my funny-voiced radio characters, and that I displayed a limited understanding of human truth. He said that he was sick of *Jaggers & Crown* and that he wanted to perform comedy that would 'expose the idiocy of the world, not contribute to it'. However, like many hopeless drinkers, Sonny needed money. So it was unsurprising when he suddenly changed his mind about ITV's generous offer and agreed to meet their executive in Chas's office to sign our contract after all. And then, as I was dressing myself on the morning of the meeting, I received a phone call.

'Is that Mr Crown?' asked a woman's voice. She sounded old and highly strung. In the background I heard someone shout 'Nice One, you Nit!' in this weird screeching tone. 'I've found your number in the coat pocket of Mr Jaggers, sir. He's here in my home. I wonder if you could come and collect him?'

'Mr Jaggers is with you now? Is he all right?'

'I wouldn't say that exactly, sir, no. He's received a distressing message from his mother that has upset him terribly. And he's been at the liquor.'

Again from behind her, 'I'm in the Pink!'

'You surprise me,' I sighed, reaching for a pen. 'Not to worry dear, I'll drive straight over. What's your name?' She said her name was Hilda Hannigan and she gave me her address in Tooting. And, as I jotted that down, I remembered that Sonny's mother had been dead for five years.

Madame Hilda lived in a basement flat that you could only access by disappearing up a narrow alley. It was a miserable day in January and the weather harassed me as I rang the bell. The moment she opened the door, I didn't like what I was dealing with. She was a bangly, beady old bird, dressed in colours too bright and hippyish for her age and her eyes seemed away with the fairies. *I bet Sonny tells you all about me*, I thought.

'Ah, Mr Crown,' she said. 'Come in, do.'

'I'm in the Pink!' someone shrieked from inside, sounding distressed.

'That's him, I take it, Mrs Hannigan,' I said as I shook the rain out of my brolly before stepping across the threshold. 'He sounds awful.'

'Oh no,' she said looking amused, as she hung my coat and hat on a hook. 'Mr Jaggers is asleep on the chaise longue, in something of a stupor. That...' she said raising a finger in the air as 'Nice One, Nice One, Nice One you Nit!' was hiccupped from the living room, '...is The Admiral. He'll be delighted to meet you, Mr Crown, he adores your programme.' She led me down a creaking staircase into a room that stank of too many pets and not enough husbands, and where my comedy partner was lying face down on a dilapidated piece of furniture. He was surrounded by miniature whisky bottles, all of them empty.

'He was the worse for wear when he arrived,' the woman said, 'but he insisted on sitting for a séance. He's been visiting me for years, you see, and he's always behaved himself before.'

'Behave yourself!' someone squawked. I turned to the window and saw a parrot in a cage, shifting on its perch from one foot to another and eyeing me like it had a complaint.

'You behave *yourself*, you naughty Admiral!' chuckled Hilda. She pointed to the television and told me how much the bird enjoyed watching *Jaggers & Crown*. 'I've been trying to teach him the theme song,' she said, 'but he hasn't a musical ear.'

I went over to Sonny and crouched beside him.

'Sonny,' I said, 'it's me. I'm taking you home.' Sonny rolled over and opened his eyes. He murmured something that was difficult to hear.

'Little Kevin,' I think he said, 'and his perfidious heart.' He closed his eyes again and turned away.

'His mother's spirit came to tell him to be wary of the devil,' said Hilda, as if that should explain everything. 'She said, "don't sell your soul, Alan. Whatever you do, don't sign that contract!" Or words to that effect. I couldn't swear to it, I was in a trance at the time.' I gave her one of my looks.

'The only spirits troubling him are the ones coming out of these bottles,' I said, holding up a miniature. 'He's an alcoholic.'

'I know,' Madame Hilda sighed. 'The spirits told me.' I felt like saying, *his flipping breath should have told you, you stupid mare.* But instead I shook Sonny roughly.

'Sonny, let's go. Get up.' No response. 'Alan!' I said louder, and with that he woke again. Alan was his real name, his and his Dad's. 'We've got business now, remember? With that executive?' Sonny shook his head.

'The deal with the devil,' he slurred.

'Look,' I said. 'ITV is not the devil. I've met the executive before, his name's Barry and he's ever so nice.'

'I'm not to sign anything,' Sonny declared. 'Mummy says not to.'

'Don't be daft, Alan. Mummy says nothing. It's this bloody woman messing with your head. She's barmy, can't you see? I've met people like her before, and they're all crooks.'

'Well!' Madame Hilda cried behind me. 'Thanks ever so!'

'Listen, Alan, I'm your pal. There's a lot of money at stake here, it's a good thing. Come to the meeting. Chas is waiting.' But it was useless, he'd passed out again.

'Are you going to be much longer?' huffed Madame Hilda. 'I've another séance booked for later. The spirits won't wait for you to clear off.'

I stood up and considered the problem. Barry from ITV was due to arrive in less than thirty minutes at Chas's office with the contract but it was obvious that Sonny was in no fit state to sign anything. 'I need to use your phone, Mrs Hannigan,' I said finally.

In the corridor of the above flats was an old coin-slot telephone, where I went to dial the number of Wimold Artistes. Chas answered after half a ring.

'I'm with Sonny,' I said. 'But it's not good.' I explained that not only was it impossible for Sonny to attend the meeting but also that, if Barry from ITV should see Sonny in his current condition, the deal would be cancelled anyway.

'Nobody's cancelling anything,' Chas replied. 'Where's your Dunkirk spirit? You just phone me back in half an hour when Barry'll be here. I've an idea.'

Chas gave me my instructions and I hung up. I stood there then, in a stranger's hallway, going over things in my head. After thirty minutes of this I fed more coins into the phone and redialled the office.

'Crowny!' Wimold said. 'There you are. I'm here with Barry from ITV and we were starting to worry about you. I've been saying about how that pesky motor of yours keeps breaking down. I keep telling you to join the Automobile Association but you never listen. Anyway, it doesn't matter, he says I can sign all this without you. Hang on a sec, I'll pass you over to him.'

'Hello Kevin,' said Barry from ITV. 'It's Barry. Listen, jolly bad luck about the car trouble. Still, you'll be able to afford a nice new one in a month or two.' I told him that I looked forward to it. 'So you don't mind Chas here signing the deal on your behalf, then? It's fine with us of course but we need your permission.' I said no, I didn't mind. 'And Sonny? He's happy with this?' Oh yes, I replied. Sonny is excited about the deal. 'Good. Can I speak to him? Is he there?' I said yes, I'll just get him. There was a pause on the line for three or four seconds.

'Hello Barry. Sonny here. We haven't had the pleasure.'

'No,' replied Barry, 'but I must say I'm an enormous fan of yours. I'm so excited that you both are coming to ITV.'

'As are we, Barry. As are we.'

'Not planning on retiring from comedy, then? Because we heard rumours.'

'Oh behave yourself, Barry! You just to tell Wimold to sign the document and to open that cigar box of his. We'll see you at Elstree!' Barry laughed and the call ended.

When I returned to her living room, Madame Hilda had extended her gate-leg table and was scattering tarot cards over it, face down. Sonny was snoring gently.

'It's ever so sad,' she said quietly, 'that someone who brings so much laughter into the world should be pursued by so many demons.' I crossed the room, sat beside Sonny and stroked his hair. If she hadn't have been there, if it had just been the two of us, I would have kissed him.

'I wouldn't worry yourself about it, Mrs Hannigan,' I whispered. 'He'll be alright.'

I could hear the snap of a particular card as she turned it over. Something inside me turned to ice. 'I wasn't talking about him,' she said.

After one week of filming on their new series, Sonny Jaggers was found dead in his home, after taking an overdose of sleeping pills. In the following years Kevin struggled to maintain a television career and throughout the following decades became an increasingly marginal figure in British entertainment.

He made small appearances on daytime quiz shows but he never recaptured the glory days of *Jaggers & Crown*.

'Dead yet, Kev?' Maisie asked as she wiped a nearby table. I looked up from the paper and saw from the clock that I had passed an hour staring at page 36. My eggs had gone cold and Jingo was asleep at my feet. Apart from myself there was nobody in the café, the old gentleman had slipped off quietly. 'From the expression on your face I should say that your obituary has arrived right on time. You look like Death warmed up!'

'Not a bit, Mais,' I replied, snapping myself out of it. 'I'm just wondering what I'm going to say when I phone up this paper later on and shock them with the news that I'm still here. They've already realised their mistake most probably and are bracing themselves for a right ruddy earful.'

Maisie said, 'That's the spirit,' and took away my untouched plate. I tugged at Jingo's lead and left some coins on the side for Maisie. I didn't know what I planned to do with the rest of the day but I doubted I'd be contacting the paper. I couldn't imagine what the point would be.

'Ain't you taking your paper?' Maisie called over as the bell above the door tinkled. I had left it on the table, open at my obituary.

'No thanks, love,' I said, 'I only buy it for the cryptic crossword and today's is a toughie. You have a go.' I gave her a wink and left.

Kevin Crown never married and left no children. His death was the result of a perfidious heart.

Swimming with the Fishes

Jennifer Moore

We bought him from the pet shop on Cavalla Road, in the hope of livening up the fish tank.

'His name's John,' the shop assistant said, 'and he comes with a choice of diving suits: squid ink black or starfish red.' I liked the red one he had on best and Davy preferred the black, so in the end Mum got one of each. The shop assistant said that John would be happy to swap them on a weekly basis as long as we looked away while he was getting changed. 'He can be a bit shy like that.'

While we were there we chose a tall rock for him to sit on between dives, a tiny lilo bed and a full month's supply of nutri-flakes and oxygen pellets. Technically, it's possible to refill the air tank after every dive, using a complicated siphon and pump system, but the assistant said it was rather fiddly and John was happy enough with the pellets. He nodded his agreement and gave us a timid thumbs up.

'Can he talk?' I asked.

The shop assistant smiled and lifted him up in the palm of her hand. 'Well, John?' she said softly. 'This young lady would like to know if you can talk.'

John stood there for a moment, staring down at his flippers. Finally he nodded.

The shop assistant put him back down on the counter while she prepared his bag, half filling it with water before she lowered him in, adding a few oxygen pellets. She knotted the bag at the top and we all watched as John dived downwards, turning a neat somersault at the bottom before swimming back up to the surface to tread water. The shop assistant put her spare hand up to her mouth to shield her lips from view and whispered, 'He's quite a chatterbox when he gets going, but he can be painfully shy with strangers.'

'Anything else we should know?' asked Mum. 'We've never had a diver before.'

'Give him a couple of nutri-flakes three times a day and make sure he's got plenty of oxygen. That's it really. He'll tell you if there's anything else, I'm sure.'

John was floating on his back by the time we got him home.

'He's dead,' shouted Davy in excitement.

'I expect he's just catching his breath,' said Mum, giving the bag a little prod.

John flipped over onto his stomach and did a few slow laps of breast-stroke. 'There you are, he's fine. Let's get him into the tank shall we, before he gets too tired?'

We sank the rock in first so that he'd have somewhere to rest and then Mum undid the bag and floated it on the surface of the water.

'Just for fifteen minutes,' she told John. 'Then another fifteen with some of the tank water added to the bag to help you acclimatise, and then you're free to go.'

He nodded and dived down to the bottom of the bag for a closer look at the zebra fish who were swimming underneath. They were studiously ignoring him but John didn't seem to care. He stuck two oxygen pellets in his air tank and stayed down there for the entire half hour, miming excitable greetings to his tank-fellows. As soon as we let him out he was off with the shoal, ducking in and out of the plastic pond fern, weaving his way between the two small stragglers at the back.

John seemed happy enough in his new home, once we'd removed Davy's grinning skull from the gravel at the bottom (it took him a full fortnight to admit it was giving him nightmares), and with each passing week he grew increasingly talkative, just like the shop assistant had promised. Every afternoon at feeding time, he'd scull across on his lilo, singing the theme tune from Hawaii Five-O, and carefully raise himself up on his feet, hooking his elbows over the edge of the tank ready for a chat. I'd tell him about my day at school or the latest preparations for my dance show, and he'd fill me in on all the tank gossip, although to be honest there was rarely anything of interest to report. Sometimes he forgot to change his suit over (he admitted to me in secret that he preferred the red one too) but he was well behaved and polite and much more fun to interact with than the fish, who did nothing more than swim around in circles.

Davy was less impressed however; too much talking, he complained, and not enough action. John looked a little hurt at this but remained firm in his refusal to pinch the zebra fish's tails like Davy suggested. He didn't fancy the sound of the plastic shark with the self-opening jaws that Davy wanted to buy either.

'You don't like skulls,' sulked Davy. 'You don't like sharks. What do you like?'

'I just like diving,' said John, 'it's all I've ever wanted to do.' His gaze dropped to his flippers and he gave a shy smile. 'I'd really love a shipwreck to explore,' he said. 'They had one in the tank next to me at the shop.' He gave a dreamy sigh. 'It was wonderful– there was coral growing over the sides and a treasure chest on the deck. When the lid was open you could see the gleaming gold and jewels inside and thick streams of bubbles.'

'Sounds rubbish,' said Davy.

'It sounds great. I'll ask Mum,' I promised.

Back at the pet shop on Cavalla Road we bought a plastic wreck with a bubble-powered lid and a tiny pair of non-mist goggles in red, to match John's favourite suit. His original pair got a little steamed up sometimes which made it hard to see where he was swimming. Davy wanted to buy an electric eel to 'spice things up a bit' but the shop assistant explained that they didn't make very good tank-fellows due to their electrical impulses, their carnivorous diet and the fact that they could grow up to two and a half metres in length. All of which only made Davy want one more, of course. He could save up his pocket money, he told us, or maybe get one as an early birthday present. Mum just sighed and told him not to be so silly. Luckily John was safely back at home with the zebra fish (we'd left him doing laps of the tank, too excited to keep still) because the merest hint of an eel for a tank-mate would have been enough to give him bad dreams for nights on end.

I snuck a packet of chocolate flavour Diver Drops onto the counter when we went to pay and Mum just raised her eyebrows and did that funny sideways lip stretch. She paid for them along with the rest of the shopping, without saying a word.

'How come she gets to buy a wreck, new goggles and some treats,' grumbled Davy 'and I don't even get one little eel?'

'They're not for me,' I told him, 'they're for John.'

'You wanted a diver too,' Mum reminded him.

'But that was before I knew how rubbish he'd be,' grumbled Davy. 'All he does is swim around all day.'

'Well what did you expect?'

'Couldn't we get him a gun or something? What about a harpoon?'

'He's good company when you get to know him properly,' I said. 'He's got loads of interesting stories.' That last bit was a lie, but I felt duty-bound to defend him. 'Maybe if you tried being a bit nicer to him...'

'What about a crab?' asked Davy. 'Can we get a crab?'

John was thrilled with the shipwreck (or the sunken galleon, as he called it), and his new goggles.

'*I can see clearly now the steam has gone,*' he sang, as he emerged from the water to claim his chocolate Diver Drop. '*I can see all obstacles in my way...*'

'What's it like down there?' I asked him. 'Any pirate skeletons lurking beneath deck? Or a giant squid hiding in the hull?'

John giggled. 'Just jewels and gold coins. I wanted to bring you a diamond but I couldn't pry it loose.' He held up his hands to reveal big red scratches across his palms.

I blushed. 'Thank you for trying. That was very sweet.'

I hadn't even heard Davy come into the room until he started chanting, 'John's got a girlfriend, John's got a girlfriend.' Despite my best efforts I could feel my cheeks getting even redder.

John looked uncomfortable too. 'I'd better be getting back,' he said quietly. 'I want to have an explore of the port holes down on the starboard side. See if I can find another way in.'

'There's nothing *to* explore,' said Davy scornfully, having examined the wreck carefully on the way home from the pet shop. 'It's made of polyresin, whatever that is. Wouldn't you rather have a crab? You could ride him like a cowboy.' He made a slapping motion with his right hand while holding invisible reins in his left.

John shivered. 'No thanks. I'm happy with my galleon.' He flipped himself backwards off the edge of his lilo and retreated back down to the depths.

'What a wimp,' said Davy as the diver changed direction to avoid the approaching zebra fish. 'An electric eel would have been much more fun.'

John didn't seem to tire of his new tank toy. Sometimes he pretended he was Jacques Cousteau exploring the Madhia wreck. Sometimes the wreck was the Mary Rose, and at other times the seventeenth-century Spanish galleon Concepcion. On the odd morning when I was downstairs before he woke up I would hide new treasures in the wreck for him to find: a five pence piece; the silver cross from my christening necklace; an old chocolate coin that had glued itself to the bottom of the sweet tin with something red and sticky. I liked to watch the excitement and triumph on John's face when he hauled his treasures up to the surface to show me. It was a good game while it lasted: when Mum caught me sinking a steel nut I'd found on the garage floor I got a mini-lecture about water quality and the delicate chemical balance needed for keeping healthy fish. There were no more treasure sinkings after that.

There was another lecture (not quite so mini this time) for Davy, after Mum caught him taking pot shots at John with his water pistol. Davy claimed it was just a game and John had been enjoying it as much as he had but the purple water-pressure bruise on John's arm when he rolled up his wet-suit sleeve told a different story.

'What's the point of having a pet if you can't play with it?' asked Davy.

'John is a "he" not an "it",' corrected Mum.

'Can't we get a dog?'

'You know we can't,' said Mum wearily. 'Your sister's allergic to animal hair.'

Davy thought for a moment. 'What about a snake then?'

Mum shivered. 'We're not getting a snake. Or a lizard or a tortoise or a spider. I think eight fish and John are quite enough, thank you very much.'

'But they don't do anything,' complained Davy. 'You can't train a fish or get it to fetch sticks. And as for John...' He glared at the little diver who was rolling his sleeve back down and preparing himself for another dive.

'Shh,' I said. 'You'll hurt his feelings.'

'Why don't you think of some games you can play with him?' suggested Mum. 'Some non-violent ones. You could teach him 'I Spy' or charades.'

Davy looked unimpressed. 'Something beginning with L— loser.' He put his hand to his forehead in an L-shape. Mum slapped it back it down.

'That's enough,' she said. 'Now I've got to help your sister with her costume for the dance show on Saturday. I expect to find you playing nicely with John when I get back. No guns, no sharks, no nets. Do you understand?'

Davy gave a sullen nod.

We can't have been gone more than quarter of an hour, just long enough for Mum to pin the chicken wings into position on my yellow leotard and put my hair up into a bun to fit the feathered band around my head. But it was long enough.

'How did you get on?' asked Mum when we got downstairs. Davy was on the sofa reading a football magazine.

'Okay,' he shrugged.

'Are you both friends now?'

Davy shrugged again. 'We were playing nicely together until he went off on his own.'

'Where is he?' I asked, scanning the tank for a glimpse of red wetsuit. The wreck lay still and empty at the bottom. 'John?' I called, peering through the fronds of plastic fern. 'Are you hiding?'

'He just disappeared halfway through the game,' said Davy, looking increasingly shifty.

'What game was this exactly?' asked Mum, pulling Davy's magazine down so she could see his face properly.

Davy didn't answer.

'I said what game was it?' Mum's voice had gone hard and spiky. I was still staring into the tank, still hoping to spot a tell-tale glimpse of red amongst the green. There was a horrible, sick feeling growing at the bottom of my stomach.

'Toilet Tsunami,' he mumbled at last.

'Oh Davy,' said Mum, the colour draining out of her cheeks, 'please tell me you didn't...'

'It's not my fault he's such a rubbish swimmer. I told you we should have got an eel.'

I ran upstairs to see, locking the bathroom door behind me. I couldn't believe he was gone. I wouldn't believe it.

I was still there, still staring into the bowl, still waiting for John to come surfing back up the U-bend when Mum got back from the pet shop.

'Please open the door, sweetheart,' she begged. 'There's someone here who wants to meet you. His name's Finn.'

Charles Lambert is one of two authors in this volume to have also appeared in our first anthology, Various Authors. *When you read 'Pretty Vacant', I think you'll see why we've asked him back so soon.*

Pretty Vacant

Charles Lambert

Three days after my fifteenth birthday my father kisses me on the lips, pinches my left cheek until it hurts, says he'll always love me and flies off to Madagascar with his new girlfriend, Mia. I've seen her once or twice in the back of his car or waiting outside his secretary's office with a magazine, *Bella* or *Chi*, chewing the inside of her mouth, and I've wondered who she is. Someone who needs a job and is scared she might not get it, I thought at first, so I was half right; living with my father is a sort of job. My mother's pretended not to notice. She's getting ready to move into our summer house near Alghero.

The next day she tells me I'm going to spend the entire summer in a college in England, to perfect my command of the language. We're in the dressing room just off her bedroom, gold and crimson striped sofas and pouffes, Chinese carpet, a massive chandelier. A friend of hers decorated it for her last winter, but she isn't happy. She's thinking of doing it over in Boston colonial, she says, and I wonder how many colonists had whole rooms filled with designer clothes. I cry and shout and sweep some underwear off the dressing table onto the floor, because tantrums usually work in my house, but she closes her face, snap! like a fan, and tells me there's nothing further to discuss. I know she's lying; she knows I know. I already have a perfect command of English. I'm leaving the room when she says: Besides, you might be kidnapped if you stay in Italy, like that girl at your school. What was her name? Enrica, I say. Her surname, says my mother. Whose daughter was she? This dreadful envious country, all people think about is other people's money. No wonder everyone's leaving.

English. Kidnapping. My father says you should never use more than one excuse, that excuses lose their value the more there are.

The coaches pull into the college drive a few minutes before midnight. I'm curled up in a window seat, legs tucked beneath my bottom, my left leg almost dead. I see a large dark door with a light above it and an arc of yellowish gravel. The door swings open and a woman with tight blue-purple hair and a long beige cardigan comes out, clutching a clipboard. The other kids push towards the driver, crushed in the aisle and down the steps, but I stay where I am, three rows from the back, my head down low. I watch them shuffle into line, and the woman in the cardigan calling out names and ticking them off. My name is called out. Nothing happens, and Cardigan looks up, repeats it, glances around.

They have to come and fetch me out. Cardigan says I must be tired. When I don't answer, she purses her lips and ticks me off with the rest. We're taken up a flight of old wooden stairs, carrying our own cases. I'm in a room at the end of a corridor with two other girls: a German more or less my own age with three tennis rackets in monogrammed blue leather cases, who says her name is Birgitte; and a fat girl from Spain in a blouse and short pink skirt and ankle socks with frills round the top. We watch while another woman opens drawers and wardrobe doors and mimes the putting away of clothes. When she leaves we stay where we are in the middle of the bare cold room, avoiding one another's eyes. Then Birgitte wrinkles her nose and makes a snorting noise, like a horse, and the fat girl starts to cry. Nobody says anything. I'm not shy, I just don't want to talk. After a minute or two, the fat girl stops snivelling and slumps on her bed, then kicks off her shoes with a sullen jerk and glances down at them, in the middle of the floor. She says something I don't catch in Spanish. She's used to having someone pick them up, I think, and smile to myself. Fat chance.

I'm almost asleep when she squeals *Araña! Araña!* I get out of bed and open the curtains to get some light. She's huddled in the bottom corner of her bed against the wall, pointing at her pillow. Birgitte watches me with half-closed eyes as I cross the room and pick up the pillow. What is it? she says and you can hear her German accent. She says there's a spider, I tell her. *Araña*, the Spanish girl sobs hopelessly. I shake the pillow and punch it. *Niente ragno*, I say and then, to Birgitte, no spider, look, she must have dreamt it. The Spanish girl begins to weep tears of relief and gratitude. She grabs my hand and presses it to her face. I put my arm round her shoulder. *Va bene, tutto va bene.*

Next morning, she gets up close to my ear and whispers her name, Pilar, like a secret and follows me into the bathroom, watching me as I wash my face and brush my teeth and hair, then back into the bedroom where we dress. Ignoring Birgitte, she chatters in Spanish about her family, her cats, her friends; she doesn't speak a word of English. She's frightened of everything, apart from me. She's terrified of Birgitte, who tells her she mustn't speak Spanish, but English, because learning English is what our parents have paid for.

We go downstairs to a room with long wooden tables and benches pushed up against them and the sick smell of boiled milk. I ask her how old she is. Twelve, she says. She won't eat the food dished out to us, bacon and scrambled eggs, caked and greyish-yellow, but fills her mouth with slices of doughy white buttered bread. When Cardigan comes round and asks us how we are she reaches for my hand under the table, her fat face anxious and resentful. We're fine, I say. Cardigan looks at me a second time, remembering who I am.

Enrica was released after forty days in a cave in Calabria somewhere. Three men bundled her into a car as she came out of her piano lesson, somewhere near Porta Venezia. They drove her down south in the back of a lorry. She didn't tell me this herself. It was all in the paper as soon as she was released. But it didn't say how much the ransom was; it never does. There was a photograph on television of her holding up a copy of *La Stampa* so you could see the date: 17 March 1977. She looked as though she'd been crying. She's lucky they didn't cut something off, to send to her parents. An earlobe, a finger. They do that sometimes. I don't think I could stand it.

'Okay, let's start.' The teacher smiles, picks up a clipboard. She's dressed like a car mechanic in blue overalls, a T-shirt, laced-up green boots. 'What's your name?' she says, slowly, in a clear loud voice. We're being questioned one by one, like suspects.

'Francesca. That's my first name. My surname's Contini.' I spell this out, quickly, to show that I can. C-O-N-T-I-N-I. She looks me over, sizes me up.

'I'm Elizabeth,' she says. 'I teach the top class here, so I expect I'll be teaching you. Where are you from, Francesca?'

'Milan, in Italy. My family has an apartment in the centre, near the Castello Sforzesco.'

'How beautiful,' she says. I recognise her now. She's the one who showed us where to put our clothes.

'Not everyone thinks it's beautiful. Milan, I mean.'

'Perhaps they don't know it very well,' she says. 'You've studied English quite a lot before this, haven't you?'

'Yes. I am English, practically. I don't know why I'm here.'

She looks up from her clipboard, amused. I want to cry. 'Have you got any brothers and sisters?' she says.

'No. I'm an only child.' Not for much longer. Mia's expecting a baby; my mother told me before I left. Your father's *puttana* is pregnant, she said, packing her shoes into their special case. Why are you taking so many shoes? I asked. You're going to the summer house. My mother laughed, but I could see I'd annoyed her. You can never take too many shoes, she said. I wonder sometimes what they teach you girls at school.

'I had an English nanny,' I say. 'She came from Andover.' Elizabeth pulls a face I'm not supposed to notice, her head down over the clipboard, but I can see she's impressed. Still, I wish I'd kept my mouth shut. I'm not sure if I pronounced Andover right.

The rest of the day, Pilar attaches herself to me, her hand in mine, her damp arms clinging to my waist or neck, wanting to be kissed. The others leave us alone, but I don't care. Being with Pilar is better than being by myself because nobody bothers me. Even Birgitte, after trailing behind us for a while and talking to me in her odd stiff English, has wandered off with the other Germans. We walk round the school and the swimming pool and the empty gym. Later we're taken into the town by a sports teacher and shown where to buy ice creams. He says it's good practice for our English, though most of them just point at the picture by the fridge and hand over notes. Pilar has no money with her, so I pay for us both. We dawdle until we're left behind on our own. Outside a café, a gang of boys watches as we walk by, making comments I can't quite hear. As soon as we're past them, I turn round and stare at them until they look away, except for one, who waves. I don't wave back. The sky's full of fat grey clouds. When it starts to rain Pilar wants to shelter, but I'd rather get wet. I tell Pilar about my mother's house in Alghero, the private beach, my uncle's new yacht. She doesn't understand it all, but I don't care. It's better that way.

In our room, as soon as the lights are out, with Birgitte's breathing a throaty drone, Pilar comes over to my bed and slips in beside me and I don't have the heart to kick her out.

Morning break the second day, I run across the garden to the big house, up the stairs and into my bedroom. I open my wardrobe door and unzip a side pocket on my case, pull out a plastic bag and cigarette papers. Cross-legged on the floor, I roll two joints from the grass in the bag, then put it away and slip the joints into the back pocket of my jeans. I only notice Pilar has followed me as I close the wardrobe. Get back to the classrooms, I say. I'll be there in a minute. She swings round in a huff and goes downstairs.

The boys are outside the café. Their English is odd, but I understand when they ask me where I come from and who I am. I don't tell the truth, it's more fun to lie. I've done this before, pretended to be someone else, with foreign tourists or boys from Cologno and Sesto Marelli, who hang around Fiorucci on Saturday afternoons when I'm supposed to be riding. I tell them my name's Marina, the name of my closest friend at school.

The tallest one, the one who waved yesterday, says I sound like a swimming pool. He wants to know how old I am. I look at him, let him wait. His hair's shaved off at the sides, the bit between his nostrils looks red and sore. He's got a stud and three silver rings in the lobe of his right ear; the top hole's gone septic. There's a ragged scab and a bead of pus the size of the stud. He's wearing a T-shirt that's gone at the neck and tight too-short black jeans. He looks as though he hasn't eaten in days.

'Seventeen,' I say, and he grins, because he knows I'm lying.

We go down a side passage between the café and a shop, two boys in front of me and two behind. I feel like someone rich, surrounded by bodyguards. The passage comes out onto a narrow road, without shops. A woman is sweeping the outside steps of her house. She stops and watches us walk past, then shakes her head. I don't need summer school, I think with a surge of joy I can't crank down, I've made my own friends. We stop in a bus shelter with no glass in the windows and a broken wooden bench. The tall one goes in first, I follow. I give him the first joint and watch while he lights it with a match. He draws on it, coughs, his face going purple, his neck veins standing out.

'Fucking hell,' he says. 'It's grass.'

'It's pure.'

'It is that.' He passes the joint to one of the others, who ducks in beside us. I wait until it comes to me. I hold the smoke down and look at the cracked floor of the bus shelter and see my mother walking down the path from the villa to the beach, her feet in glittering sandals, her damp hair twisted up in a bun. I see my father with Mia in some bar on a terrace with lemurs and palm trees, his hand on her belly feeling their child, and I hope they never come back. I hope they die.

A car pulls up outside the bus shelter. The sports teacher from our table at the college jumps out, then grabs me too hard by the top of the arm. 'You ought to be in class,' he says. I shake him off. I want to run but he's blocking my way, his football whistle dangling round his neck. I can smell his sour fresh sweat. As he drags me out to the car, I smile at the tall one. 'Ciao.'

'Yeah, right,' he says. The other boys snigger. 'Ciao.'

After lessons that afternoon I go back to the café, even though I've been told not to leave the college again that day. The tall one isn't there but his friends are sitting at a table with empty cups on it, and an ashtray and a newspaper folded open to show a woman with her breasts out.

'You looking for Gary?'

I shrug, then nod. 'It doesn't matter though,' I say.

One of them scratches his leg at the top, by the crotch, and grins. 'We'll tell him you called.'

When Pilar creeps over to my bed again, I don't care if Birgitte's awake or not. It's none of her business. I move to make room and she climbs in and curls against me, her hair in my face, my hair in hers. I stroke it away, whether mine or Pilar's makes no difference, I think, sniffing the eucalyptus scent of the same shampoo, because Pilar insisted I use the bottle her grandmother bought from a famous shop in Madrid. I feel her breathing slow down. I hug her close. She sleeps, her mouth open on my neck. Pilar is also an only child.

Gary is waiting for me outside the college. When I come out, he drops his cigarette and crushes the stub beneath his foot. How stupid he looks, pretending to be a man, but I'm glad all the same that he knows where to find me.

'You were looking for me,' he says. 'You didn't come back.'

'I wasn't looking for you.'

I walk off quickly, away from the town. I want to get away before Pilar comes out of the school bank. That's what Cardigan calls the room where she gives us our pocket money. She sits behind a desk with a tray of cards and a cash box. When she looks at my card, she makes a smug little smile and I know she likes it that I've got so much money, it reflects on her college. I've decided to take out five pounds, the same amount, each day, but never spend more than a pound or two. I'll keep the extra money in my case, with the grass. It makes me feel safe to know it's there. It means I can always get away.

When Pilar's turn came the first time, Cardigan couldn't believe her eyes. She checked in a book, then tapped her pen on the desk and turned to the sports teacher, David, because it's all first names here, we're all the best of friends. He's there to protect the money. He looked at the card and whistled. How much do you want? said Cardigan, her voice all tight and disapproving but it was wasted on Pilar, who didn't understand. I whispered and she shook her head. *Nada*, she said. I decide that, tomorrow, I'll tell her to ask for five pounds too.

Gary and I are already round the corner when Pilar calls out. I grab his T-shirt and tug. 'Come on,' I say. 'Quick!'

We run for a few minutes, then turn into a park. Gasping for breath, we dart down a path. I graze my arm on a bush. 'Look,' I say, 'blood,' in a ghoulish voice. Gary doubles over and I see how his hair has been hacked around at the back. He's done it himself, I think, standing between two mirrors with a pair of scissors, cutting away great lumps of hair.

'I haven't got any grass this time. I didn't expect to see you.'

He grins. 'You trust Gary,' he says. 'Come on.' He takes me past streets of houses in dark red brick, their doors directly on the pavement, with painted steps. I let him lead me down one street, then another, always a step or two behind. I watch his thin legs in the tight black trousers and his narrow shoulders under the greyish cotton of his T-shirt. I look at the spikes of dirty blond hair bobbing up and down as he walks before me with an awkward, musical bounce.

'I'm in a squat,' he says. 'It's all mine at the moment, 'cause everyone's gone to Wales. They're living in this cowshed doing acid. They're fucking mad. They wanted me to go with them, but I hate the fucking country. It smells like shit.'

We walk through a gate and into the bare hall of a house, and I'm feeling short of breath and free as he opens a door on the first floor landing.

There's a mattress beneath the window, T-shirts and jeans thrown on it, and cushions behind the door, the kind with little mirrors sewn into them. Across the wall someone has sprayed *The Road of Excess Leads to the Palace of Wisdom* in red paint. I look at the books on the windowsill while Gary plugs in a kettle in the corner. Kerouac. Comics. Something called *The Magus*, its pages falling out. The Pauper's Cookbook. Carlos Castaneda. There's a poster pinned to the wall, of four men in an alley. One of them has a T-shirt with *Brigate Rosse* written on it and the five-pointed star.

'Why is he wearing that T-shirt?'

'That's Joe Strummer,' he says. 'The Clash.'

I ask again. All at once I feel homesick. The wall of the building I live in had a red-pointed star for half a day, before it was painted over.

'The Red Brigades? They're Italian, right?'

'Yes.'

'They're brilliant.' He starts to rub his bare arms. He's so thin and pale I feel sorry for him, and slightly envious.

'We can't go round the centre of Milan at weekends,' I say. 'It's too dangerous. There are soldiers everywhere.'

'That's what we need here,' says Gary, eyes gleaming. 'Something real.' He picks up a cardboard box of singles. 'Listen to this,' he says, taking one out and putting it onto the deck by the bed. He stands up and starts to bellow out the words. Vacant. Oh so vacant. His heels together, both arms pressed to his sides, he leaps into the air, rigid as a board. I've never seen anything like it. For a second I think he's having a fit. I burst into hysterical laughter, which spurs him on. 'Come on,' he shouts over the music, 'I'll teach you to pogo.'

This time I'm back before anyone notices, except Pilar. She darts a look of hatred at me through the glass walls of the gym, then runs across as I walk through the open door and sit on a pile of itchy orange mats, flinging herself across me and knocking the breath out of my lungs. I push her off and she squats at my side, pouting and rolling the hem of my T-shirt into a sausage. She reminds me of someone, I can't think who. David, the sports teacher, looks across from the wall frame, gives me a smile, walks over. He takes Pilar by the upper arms and lifts her off me. She's wriggling to be put down but he winks and says, What you need is a bit of exercise, Tubby. She screams to be put down, but I tell her to be good and that I'll be back soon. I leave the gym and go to my room. I'm still fairly stoned, though Gary's resin isn't up to much.

Elizabeth is standing by the wardrobe.

'What's this?' she says. She's holding my plastic bag in her hand.

'It's mine.'

'It's drugs, isn't it?'

'It's grass. It isn't "drugs".'

'And what do you know about "drugs"?' she says, imitating me. I almost start to laugh. I'm not afraid of you, I think, my heart pumping.

'As much as you do,' I say. 'At least.' The skin around her mouth and jaw line is tight, and it takes me a moment to realise she's also trying not to laugh. I say: 'My father keeps cocaine in this little silver box in his bathroom. He thought I wouldn't know what it was. I've done it a few times. There was lots, he never realised, he goes there with his business colleagues and they sniff it together. And there's a girl in my class at school who uses heroin with her boyfriend and I smoked some with her once. It's not that special. She says it's no good if you smoke it. But I don't really want to try it, not with a needle, I mean. I think that's stupid.'

'I'm not sure you should be telling me all this,' says Elizabeth, startled, still struggling not to smile. I'm not sure either. 'It's embarrassing enough as it is.'

'Why? Because you opened my suitcase without my permission?'

Elizabeth looks flustered, then apologetic. 'This really wasn't my idea,' she says.

I shrug. 'Somebody's been a spy. That's all right. I bet I know who it was.' Pilar, I think, getting her own back for being left behind.

'That doesn't matter,' says Elizabeth. She holds up the bag. 'But I don't really think I can leave this with you.'

'You can take it then,' I say. 'As a present. You can smoke it with the other teachers.'

Elizabeth starts to laugh. 'I don't think I'm allowed to accept presents.'

'Well, you can't throw it away. It's worth a lot of money. It's very good grass. It's the finest quality.'

'That's not the point, Francesca.'

'Yes, it is.'

Cardigan calls me into her office after lessons the next morning. I think she's been told about the grass, and I'm ready to tell her to fuck off, because what have I got to lose? She can't send me home, there's no one there. I wish she would, I'd rather be alone in Milan in any case. But all she wants to do is thank me for looking after Pilar, who isn't an easy child; I've been so sweet with her, she says. She tells me I'm an asset and very mature for my years and she hopes I'll be just as much help on the next course, after Pilar and the others have all gone home. This is how I discover I'm the only person booked in for the entire summer. I'm some kind of fixture. I stare at her with loathing until she starts to cough and says I should run along now, or I'll miss lunch, and I'm far too thin as it is.

As if I'm going to eat. Thank God there's Gary, I think. Especially now my grass has gone.

On Sunday, Elizabeth asks me to help sort out the library, three boxes of dog-eared paperbacks to be put on shelves at the back of the classroom. We're kneeling side by side on the floor as she hands the books to me and I stand them on the shelves in alphabetical order. I start singing to myself, quietly, so that Elizabeth won't hear. It's a song called *Samarcanda*, about being caught out by death. After a moment, she starts to hum along and I burst into tears.

'I shouldn't be here. I don't deserve to be here,' I say, as soon as I can speak. 'I'm being punished for being alive.' I know how melodramatic that sounds, but I can't stop myself. Anyway, it's true. I am being punished. Yet I feel ashamed, as though I've betrayed myself.

Elizabeth puts down the book she's holding, reaches across and squeezes my shoulder.

'Don't be unhappy,' she says. 'You needn't be, you know.'

'My mother wants me to be unhappy. That's why I'm here. She'd rather I spent the whole fucking summer in this place than anywhere near her. She told me I was a dead weight. I hate her. And him. I hate them both.'

'That's a terrible thing to say.'

'I don't care. It's true.'

'I don't mean what you said. What your mother said. It's terrible to tell a child she isn't wanted.'

Elizabeth hugs me, then holds me away until her eyes are staring into mine, exactly level, as if we are equals and alone. For a moment I think she's about to kiss me and wonder what I'll do if she does. But she lets me go and begins to speak.

'My mother sent me away, when I was seventeen. To this family in Geneva she'd found through an agency. They were South American, Colombian, and incredibly rich, with one spoilt child they couldn't stand that I was supposed to look after, a bit like Pilar, but younger. They had three other servants, Spanish, a maid and a butler and a chauffeur, who were treated worse than I was. I broke an ornament once and she locked me in my room without food. They took my passport off me and wouldn't let me have it back. It sounds ridiculous now but I was so miserable. One day I'd had enough and I burst into tears, like you just did. I was in the kitchen with the Spanish people, they were sweet, they looked after me because I was younger, I suppose. They gave me something to drink and hugged me until I stopped. Then the woman led me out of the kitchen and took me upstairs and into the bedroom of the wife, then through into her dressing room, which was enormous, at least twice the size of my bedroom, all wardrobes and little silk chairs against the wall. I'd never seen anything like it. And she went over to the laundry basket and opened it up and pulled out a pair of knickers, beautiful silk knickers, from the top. She lifted them up in the air then held them out to show me and I saw they were dirty at the back, you know. She sniffed. She dropped them into the basket with contempt. And you know what she said? *Mierda.* I nearly died with laughter.'

'Why weren't you at school?' I say. 'You were only seventeen.'

Elizabeth grins. 'I'd been expelled,' she says. 'For bad behaviour.'

It's Gary's idea to kidnap Pilar. It starts when I tell him about her underwear, I don't know why, maybe I'm thinking about what Elizabeth has told me. How all of it is hand-sewn from apricot silk, with tiny almost invisible stitches and ribbons and bits of ivory-coloured lace, and he says, How did they get all that money? Where did it come from? I don't know, I say. I suppose they're just rich. What, like your father is *just* rich? My father isn't that rich, I say, although of course, compared to Gary, he is, we all are. Gary's parents have thrown him out and he lives in his empty squat on what he can earn by working in a chicken factory weekends and on what he steals. Most of his books are ripped off from charity shops. He's given me a ring he took from a jeweller's; he says it's too small for his fingers. It's Indian silver, it leaves a black mark on the skin. I like the black mark more than the ring.

'She's never done anything to you,' I say.

'Her class has,' he sneers. We're on his mattress together, I'm wondering why he hasn't tried to kiss me. When he's angry his lips curl back and I can see his canine teeth, longer and sharper than the rest. Who else will love you? I think. You're skinny and poor and scabby. I'm worried that no one will, ever. No one deserves not to be wanted. 'It's not her, it's what she stands for, isn't it? There's nothing personal about it.'

'You can't kidnap her whole class, though, can you?' I say. I pause, then giggle, because I still think he's joking. 'You're right. You'll have to kidnap her.'

'I won't hurt her,' he says. He sounds annoyed, as though I've chosen to be stupid. I notice he hasn't said *wouldn't*. I'm worried suddenly.

'You won't. But kidnapping will. She'll be terrified. She'll just start crying and crying. She'll never stop. All she ever does is cry.' I might be worried, but it still gives me a thrill to talk about Pilar like this. I wonder what my father would do if I were kidnapped, if he would care, how much my life would be worth to him.

'I know,' I say. 'You could kidnap me.'

'Oh yeah,' says Gary.

'No, really, you could,' I say, excited. 'You could keep me here. We could write the ransom note together. My father's got money, lots of it. He'd pay. It'd serve him right. He'd have to fly back from Madagascar and ruin his holiday.' Perhaps his girlfriend would lose the baby, I think, with the shock.

Gary struggles to his feet, tipping the ashtray over the bed. 'You'd be no good. You'd break under interrogation,' he says. I start to laugh.

'Look at the mess you've made.' He stares at me, not sure how to take this. He's told me already I've got a posh voice and I was amused, I thought my voice was normal and that everyone spoke English as I did, in England at least. But Gary tells me I'm wrong. I sound what he calls stuck up. When he talks about class, he's talking about me, about my class. He sinks on his haunches and scrapes the ash up with his hands into a gritty pile. Ashamed of what I am, I catch him by the wrist. I bend my head towards his, then tug him over until he's only inches away. He doesn't resist when I kiss his cheek, and then his mouth.

It's easy after that. I don't think he's ever had sex before, not really. I help him take off his jeans, pulling them over his feet while he giggles, embarrassed. He's wearing green nylon underpants that need a wash, and white socks. I tug at his pants and he lifts his bottom from the bed while I slide them off. His dick is stiff already. When I sit on top of him, still dressed, he squirms and says Marina, with a sort of question in his voice, and I have to remember that's my name; I've told him a lie and now I'm stuck with it. I take off my T-shirt and he reaches up and touches my breasts. I almost squeal because his hands are cold, but then I cover them with mine. He's grinning stupidly. Yes, I say, I don't know why, nor to what. I try not to think of my father's hands on Mia as Gary fumbles with the buttons of my jeans and pushes his fingers deep down inside until he can feel me. I look at the white skin and the pale raised veins of his wrist, bent round and up.

It's when I see Pilar dolled up in a specially made party dress, all frills and sequins, with her pearl earrings and necklace, like a middle-aged woman that's been shrunk down and squashed, that I realise who she reminds me of when she pouts. She's being teased to the point of tears by a couple of French boys before the pathetic Saturday disco and she looks like my mother, padded out with puppy fat and still a child, but the mouth is the same, the same full lower lip sticking out and the angry spiteful eyes. She looks like my mother when she can't get her own way.

She dances with me all the time, she wants me to swing her round. I'm sick to death of her but she's also protection from everyone else. The other kids can't stand her. There's a pretend bar in the corner of the gym, with David and another sports teacher dressed like waiters pouring out watery orange squash. The music's the sort we get in discos at home. Donna Summer. Boney M. I think of Gary and the music he plays me and I want to pogo. When I leave the gym for a minute, Pilar runs out, red in the face, her new dress sweat-dark under the arms. She stamps her feet. Fuck off, you spoilt little bitch, I say in English, and there it is again, my mother's pout, and I wish I'd said it to her, and not Pilar.

After the disco, I tell Pilar she's a spy and a traitor. I tell her I'll never trust her again, in Italian, of course, a sort of baby Italian so that she'll understand enough of it, and she does understand because her bottom lip trembles and she starts to cry and say that it wasn't her, she hasn't said anything to anyone. She stands there shaking her head, then grabs my arm and squeezes it, her eyes red with tears.

When she comes across to me that night and begs to be let into my bed, I tell her to leave me alone, and I can see Birgitte smirking as Pilar slumps to the floor beside me in her beautiful rose pink nightdress with satin ribbons round the neck and arms, and whines oh please oh please oh please Francesca. Just leave me in peace, I hiss. Then she starts to claw and tug at the sheet and go on about what her mother and father will do to me if I don't look after her and how much they love her and, without really knowing what I'm doing, I reach down and slap her face with the back of my hand, the way my mother sometimes does to me. She falls back, shocked into silence, and I feel ashamed of myself. But that soon passes. You little traitor, I whisper to myself. I thought I could trust you.

And now the idea of kidnapping Pilar is more than a joke. We sit and scheme in Gary's bedroom, our heads together as he rolls and passes the joint to me, as I roll another one and pass it back. I tell him about Enrica, what happened to her, the snatch, the cave, the photograph with the paper to show she's still alive. Gary makes notes and drawings and diagrams, which amuse me, I don't know why, perhaps because they make no sense. And then, we lie together on the mattress, our bare arms touching, and sometimes he holds my hand and I feel safe with him, grown up, and dangerous too. We don't fuck again, I don't think Gary wants to. I don't know what I want. Sometimes I think I'm so far out of myself with anger that nothing makes any sense. Nothing seems real except smoking and holding hands. Sometimes I wonder if I'm pregnant, like Mia, and what I'll do.

We only have a week left before the first course ends and Pilar goes back to Spain. Gary wants to know what we do, from breakfast to bedtime. We've ruled out mornings because Pilar and I are both in lessons and every move we make is watched, even during break. The afternoons are best. We're free to leave the school in groups, as long as there's an older child, and I'm one of the oldest there, and Cardigan trusts me, with Pilar at least. The afternoon starts at two and goes on till supper at half past six. That gives us four and a half hours before she's missed, although the time isn't that important; she won't be going any farther than Gary's room. What's essential is that she might have covered a much greater distance, otherwise the police will find us immediately. Gary has spoken to someone he knew at school, who lives in a squat in Birmingham. His friend thinks it's really cool, says Gary. He'll make the first phone call to the school. The problem is how to get her away from me without my seeming involved in any way.

'You could knock her out,' says Gary. 'Hit her over the head with something.'

'Be serious,' I say, 'I might kill her. Anyway, I think she'd notice.'

'Well you can't bring her round here yourself.'

'No,' I say, 'but I could bring her close. I could take her to the park. We could play some kind of game, I don't know, I'll make something up with blindfolds and holding hands. Then you could lead her here. By the time she has the blindfold off, it'll be too late. If you bring her in through the back, she'll have no idea where she is. She never does anyway. She practically gets lost between the bathroom and the bedroom. She's pretty vacant.'

Gary says, excited, 'I know, let's call it Operation Pretty Vacant. OPV, for short.'

'And then what?' I say. 'After she's in your room?'

'I'll wear a mask all the time. I won't let her make any noise. I'll put carpet tape over her mouth except when she's eating.'

'You can't do that. She'll go berserk.' I giggle. 'You'll pull her moustache off when you try and take it off. Besides, she can do without food for a day or two, she's really fat.'

'In any case,' Gary says, not laughing, paler than ever and serious as though we're talking about matters of life and death, not some stupid game that won't come to anything, 'it won't take long. They'll come up with the money right away, you'll see. Her parents are bound to pay up.' He's trying to convince himself, I think.

'And what about afterwards?'

'What do you mean afterwards? After we get the money?'

What I really want to know is what will happen if we do go through with it and something goes wrong. Everyone at school was sure that Enrica was dead until the photograph came out. They thought she'd been killed and thrown into a ditch and covered in lime, the way the Mafia gets rid of people it doesn't want found. Nobody liked her much, she was always talking about her clothes, her new horse, some boy she'd met at the tennis club. None of us thought *I might be the next one.* What we felt, I'm sure, although we didn't say it, was that Enrica deserved what she got.

I haven't thought about the money. 'Yes,' I say, because I can't admit this to Gary.

'Well, we'll let her go,' he says quickly. 'That's obvious. She'll have served her purpose by then.'

'And you?' I say. 'What will you do? With all that money.'

He grins. 'I could come and live in Italy with you, couldn't I? I could join the Red Brigades.'

I imagine Gary in my mother's sitting room beneath the rose-pink chandeliers, in the villa in Sardinia, with the friends I have there, tanned and fit and rich. I see his hacked-about hair and white arms, skinny and scabbed, next to theirs and I feel ashamed, as much for them as for him. I wish we'd never met.

'You'd like that, wouldn't you?' he says, and I see that he's anxious, expecting to be hurt and I can't do that, which makes me fear him a little, the hold he has.

'Yes.'

He grips my hands in his.

'You're great, you know,' he says. 'You're not like the rest.'

Pilar's told me that her parents will be home from their holiday on Wednesday, so Gary and I decide to kidnap her on Thursday afternoon. Except that I don't even think the word kidnap. Thinking it is like saying it out loud.

After lunch, I tell Pilar I have a secret, only for her, it's something she'll really like. She doesn't believe me at first, she doesn't really trust me since I slapped her. But curiosity wins. She looks around, to make sure no one can see us, then shrugs. 'Give me your hand,' I say.

The weather's dreadful, heavy skies, flurries of biting rain. We both have our raincoats on, and proper shoes. Everyone else is in the reading room or changing for gym. I'm sure no one sees us leave the school. Walking into town, I do my best to make her feel safe with me. I ask about her cat at home, and pretend to listen to what she says. Gary said I should buy her a present, something that would make her trust me all the more, so I take her to a toyshop I've seen in the precinct. I haven't decided what to buy her, but as soon as we're inside she runs across to a display of dolls. I buy her the one she wants, the biggest one, and she flings her arms around my neck and kisses me. 'I love you,' she says, in English of all things, so she has learnt something in the last four weeks. Her parents will be proud of her. It doesn't take much to win you over, I think.

Gary and I have planned this, step by step, so that nothing can go wrong, although the bad weather is an unexpected bonus. It starts to rain more heavily and we dart into a shop to shelter. It's a junk shop, full of cardboard boxes and shelves with dirty vases. A man's sitting behind a table with a display case on the top. I look inside, see covers of magazines, but he pulls a newspaper across. 'There's nothing in here for little girls,' he says. Pilar runs to the back of the shop and tugs something out from behind a stack of plastic crates filled with empty bottles.

'*Lo quiero*,' she whines. It's an old pram, curved like a boat with high wheels at the side, and a canopy to protect the baby; the sides are painted crimson and gold. It's as tall as Pilar; she has to reach up to the handle. She pulls it to the centre of the shop. It's perfect, I think. I can't believe how perfect it is. I can't wait to see Gary's face when we turn up with a pram. I ask the man how much he wants for it. He looks surprised when I pull my purse from my pocket. Pilar runs over and hugs me. 'I love you,' she says again. 'I know you do,' I say, and then, so the man can hear, 'And I love you.'

I take her to the park by a route she'll never remember. She doesn't complain about the drizzle even, just gabbles away in baby Spanish to her new doll in the pram, while I hold her arm and guide her. As soon as we're inside the park, I take her to the farthest gate, no more than fifty yards from Gary's house. By that time, the rain has stopped, and I sit on a damp wooden bench while Pilar hangs over the edge of the pram, her feet on the wheel, making idiotic noises. After ten minutes or so, I see Gary at a distance. I watch him as he skirts round the outer edge of the park until he's only feet away from us, behind the bench and concealed by bushes. I can't quite believe this is happening. I think he'll run up and say Surprise! But he just gives a high-pitched whistle, the only kind he can do, and I pull from my pocket a scarf I bought at the market three days ago, a polyester one covered in yellow and crimson flowers.

'Pilar, I've got an idea,' I say. Pilar, engrossed in her doll, doesn't answer. 'Let's play a game.' She continues to ignore me. I touch her arm, but she shrugs me off as though I don't count, as though I'm some kind of maid. That's when I think, she needs to be taught a lesson, and I'm glad. Her face is hidden by her hair as she hangs over the pram, making cooing noises at the doll. I could be anyone as I stretch across with the scarf and rapidly, before she has time to react, tie it over her eyes and knot it hard behind her head. She struggles back out of the pram and starts to stumble around, her bottom lip already trembling, her arms outstretched, while I move out of reach. We circle around each other for a moment and it isn't until she looks as though she's going to start to scream that I take a few more steps away from her and shout help, twice. Gary leaps out of the bushes and puts his hand over her mouth. She starts to kick and struggle, and I don't say another word. I watch Gary push a ball of rags in her mouth and some carpet tape across it; then, as he holds her firm, I step up and take another scarf from my pocket and tie her wrists together; slippery against the polyester, wet from rain.

Gary pulls the doll out of the pram and gives it to me, then bundles Pilar up over the edge, one hand on her neck and the other gripping her raincoat at the waist, by the belt. She fights and kicks but can't stop Gary binding her wrists and ankles with the tape. Gary pulls up the canopy and buttons down the flap that covers the other part of the pram, then waves at me silently to leave, steering the pram towards the gate. I look around to check that no one has seen us. The park's deserted, of course, because the weather's so bad. I watch Gary disappear beyond the gate, pushing the pram before him. The doll is still in my hand. I clasp it to me, suddenly cold. I stand there for ages, maybe half an hour, before turning back.

It's easier than I expected to go to the school and say what's happened. I run into the building and straight across the hall to Cardigan's office. It started to rain much more heavily as I left the park, and I'm drenched, so it isn't hard to seem upset. Water is running off my nose and chin, my hair is plastered to my head, you can't tell what are tears and what aren't; even I can't tell. I start crying almost at once, out of relief. When I bang on the door and hear her call me in, I know I look dreadful. Cardigan jumps up from her chair and puts her arms round me. 'What on earth's the matter, my dear?' she says. I wipe my face dry on her dress, then pull away from her so that she can see how distressed I am. My voice is shaking. 'I've lost Pilar. We were in the park. I don't know where she is.' And then I begin to cry for real.

The police ask me the same questions, three, four times, until my head aches, and I give the same answers, exactly. It isn't difficult. I tell them about the doll and the pram and I can see them thinking how kind I was, so that works perfectly. The only thing I say that isn't true is that I left Pilar alone for a few minutes, we were playing Hide and Seek, and when I came back she wasn't there. There was no trace of her apart from the doll, which she had left on the bench. I know she'll say that I was with her when it happened and called something out; she heard me. What I said to the police was almost the same, but not quite: that I left her with her new toy and that when I came back and found nothing there but the doll and no sign at all of Pilar, at that moment, but not before, I called her name. She heard me as the kidnapper dragged her off, that's what people will think. It's natural she'd be confused: blindfolded and gagged and carted away, although I'm not supposed to know this, not until later. Pilar will tell her story and people will think, poor girl, while still feeling sorry for me, alone in the park with nothing but the doll. No one will doubt me.

Elizabeth stays with me all evening. We sit in the teachers' room, with other teachers coming in now and then to see how I am. David tries to ask her questions, but Elizabeth pulls a face to remind him I understand every word. 'Not now,' she says, and I'm annoyed, because I want to know what's happening too, I hate being kept in the dark. Gary's friend from Birmingham must have phoned by now to say Pilar's been kidnapped. I imagine her tied up in Gary's room, the tape across her mouth, and feel sick. When Elizabeth heats some soup from a tin and tries to make me eat, I almost am. I imagine Pilar on the bare stained mattress, the ashtray and Gary's folded clothes beside her, her eyes still covered by the scarf, her mouth taped up, and I wish I could speak to Gary, help him. It's odd how close I feel to him, sitting here with Elizabeth while he sits there with Pilar, no more a mile away, not speaking in case she remembers his voice. Perhaps she's wet herself, pee soaking into the mattress. How big is Birmingham? As big as Milan? Millions of people, millions of houses. Gary's friend will have called from a telephone box. Gary told him to ask for ten thousand pounds, in used notes, but is that too much or too little? Gary insists it's the right amount, but I'm not sure. Sometimes it seems a fortune, sometimes a joke.

Later I wonder if Cardigan has spoken to Pilar's parents and what was said. Will they fly from Spain themselves, or simply send the money? And I wonder what my own parents would do if it had been me, and wish that it had been me, so that I could have put them to the test. I would have known how to lie. Gary was stupid not to trust me.

I'm taken to bed by Cardigan. As we walk up the stairs together, I ask her to tell me what's happening, but all she does is shake her head from side to side and say what a wicked world we live in. I want to say, 'It's only for the money, I know about these things. It's got nothing to do with Pilar.' But I don't.

Birgitte's already in bed. She looks at me with great damp sorrowful eyes, but also with an edge to her glance, of anxiety and suspicion, that makes me wonder how much she's guessed.

'You must not worry,' she says, in her irritating over-precise English. 'They will find Pilar.'

'I know that,' I say. 'I'm not worried.' I toss around in bed, unable to sleep. I lie there for half an hour, maybe longer, waiting for Birgitte's breathing to change, then creep along the corridor to Elizabeth's bedroom, my eyes half closed in the light. I knock, but don't wait for an answer.

She's sitting at the window, dressed in a T-shirt and knickers. I can smell she's been smoking my grass.

'You shouldn't be in here,' she says.

'I can't sleep.'

I walk across the bedroom and sit beside her on the edge of her single bed.

'Do you know what's going on?' I say. 'Is there any more news?'

'They think she's been kidnapped. They don't know why.'

'Has anyone asked for money?' To my surprise, Elizabeth shakes her head.

'What do her parents think?' I ask.

'They're flying over. They should be here in the morning. They must be sick with worry. It must be the most awful thing, to lose a child.'

I see the half-smoked joint in an ashtray on the bedside table; not really thinking, I pick it up. Elizabeth makes a rapid gesture to stop me and then, with an awkward shudder, the kind people make when they say that someone has trodden on their grave, she holds out a box of the fine wax matches we have in Italy, *cerini*, and I'm startled to see them, how strange this all is, I think, that I'm in Elizabeth's room, and there's grass and an almost empty box of *cerini*.

'What harm can it do?' she says, as if to herself. Then, to me, 'It might help you sleep.'

'Pilar told you, didn't she?' I ask. 'About the grass.'

Elizabeth shakes her head again, and I understand now why Birgitte seems so anxious about Pilar.

I stay with Elizabeth that night, the two of us lying on our backs in the same narrow bed. At one point she wriggles her arm beneath my waist and pulls me in towards her and my heart beats faster than it ever does with Gary. I wonder if Pilar felt the same when I held her against me in bed, and her nightdress slithered against my skin, and I'd wish that she would go away, because it was hot, but also that she would stay, because it was better than lying there alone. The grass makes me want to giggle. To stop myself, I try to imagine Pilar in Gary's room. I picture her with the tape across her mouth and her hands tied together behind her back. But it feels impossible to me that she should be there, like a dream that will be gone the next morning. I can't believe what I have done. I don't mean that I feel guilty and wish I hadn't. I mean that I can't believe I'm involved in any way. And then I think of Gary and wonder where he is and what he will do, and I feel such pity for him, alone as he is, and then I do feel guilty towards myself because I know that, whatever happens, I'll be all right. He doesn't even know my real name. He still calls me Marina.

The next thing I know is I'm being woken by someone stroking my cheek. I open my eyes, the room is in semi-darkness, Elizabeth is bending over me.

'Somebody just rang the main door bell,' she says. 'There must be news.'

'What time is it?'

'It's just before half past five. You'd better get back to your room before they come for you. If you don't make it, tell them you were in the bathroom. For God's sake, don't say you slept here.'

She opens the door a crack and glances out. 'Okay,' she says, and I slip past her into the corridor.

Birgitte's sitting up in bed, wide awake. I wonder how long ago she woke up.

'I hear the bell of the front door,' she says. 'Maybe it is the police again. For you.' She purses her lips in a smirk. 'Perhaps they are looking for drugs.' I'm just about to ask her what she means when Cardigan walks in.

'Can you come downstairs, my dear?'

I nod. 'I'll put on some jeans,' I say. She stands at the door and watches me and it occurs to me that she's scared. Outside the bedroom, she says: 'They want you at the police station.'

'Have they found her?'

'They won't say.'

At the police station, we are taken into a room and asked to wait. For the first time, I'm scared. If they've found Pilar, she might have told them everything. Operation Pretty Vacant. OPV, for short. When a woman in uniform comes into the room and asks us to follow her, I realise that I'm shaking.

Two people I've never seen before are standing beside a desk. The man is tall, overweight, with longish dark hair, a crumpled blue linen suit; he reminds me of my father in a way. I can see at once that he's very rich and very tired, as though these always go together. The mother, almost as tall as the man, looks the way Pilar will look in thirty years, the same round cow-like face, the jet black hair pulled back into a netted bun, eyes glistening with tears. So Pilar won't grow up to look like my mother, I was wrong about that. They stare at me as I wait to see what will happen next. They look as though they expect me to give them what they've come for, but I can't do that. Not now. It isn't up to me.

After a moment, the woman rushes forward and I think she's going to shake me, shake the nonsense out of me. That's what my nanny from Andover used to say when I'd been naughty or answered back. But what Pilar's mother wants to do is hug me to her, press my face into the soft white collar of her coat until I'm suffocating and want to push her off, but I don't, I resist. I wait until she lets me go a little, and then some more. I'm crying now, though I don't want to cry. I wish she hadn't hugged me. I wish I knew where Gary was and what he'd done.

The police woman's joined by three more of them, two from the time before and another woman, not in uniform, in a pale grey suit. They tell me they've found the pram. It's outside, in the corridor. One of the back wheels has been broken off and the sides are covered with mud.

'Yes,' I say, 'I think so,' when they ask me if it's the one I bought for Pilar. 'Where was it?' I say, but nobody answers, they just stand and look at me, waiting. 'Where did you find it?' I say. The woman in the suit says, 'Thank you, Francesca, you can go back in there,' and points to the room with Pilar's parents, as though we belong together. 'Where did you find it?' I ask again, and then: 'Where is she? Where's Pilar?' I can hear my voice getting high and scared. But nobody answers. Back in the room, I think, they're waiting to see what I know, what I'll do.

'I want to speak to Elizabeth,' I say to the woman in uniform, who's got a kind face, who saw me at the school. 'Her teacher,' she explains to the one in the suit, who thinks for a second, then shrugs. 'Well, it can't hurt,' she says, not looking in my direction, as though I'm invisible, and that's when I understand they don't trust me any more. The uniformed woman walks off and I stand and watch a man half carry, half wheel the pram away and then I'm led into a separate room and left to wait, alone, until Elizabeth arrives. I run to hug her but she doesn't want that. She flinches and I wish I'd never asked for her.

'They've been asking about a girl called Marina,' she says. Her voice has changed. 'They think she's at the school.'

'What do they want to know?'

'They think someone called Marina's involved in what's happened,' she says, in the same cold way. I've never heard her speak like this before.

'What do you think?' I ask, and then: 'What's happened?'

'I think you should tell me what you know,' she says.

I want to, but the words don't come.

'I don't know anything,' I say.

Elizabeth leaves the door open and before anyone comes to close it I see Gary taken along the corridor between two policemen. He's crying in a noisy spluttering way as though the tears are running down into his throat. The men are half holding him up, half dragging him. Then someone I can't see closes the door and I sit and wait. I wonder if they've phoned my mother and father yet, if they're on their way from Alghero and Madagascar, angry at having their holidays interrupted. I wonder if he'll bring Mia with him, pregnant, clinging, or if she's been abandoned somewhere, like a dog. A few minutes later, the woman in the suit comes in and stares at me until I turn my head away and look at the floor and my shoes. I didn't have time to put any socks on, my feet are cold. I'm shivering again.

And then I'm led back into the room where her parents are sitting on two wooden chairs against the wall, a few feet from each other. They don't love each other any more than mine do. I expect he's got his own little Mia tucked away somewhere. She's lonely and hates him. She eats too much.

They don't deserve to have children.

They're waiting for something to happen, like me.

Mischa Hiller is the author of two novels, Sabra Zoo *and* Shake Off, *both of which are well worth seeking out (you'll find details at the back of this volume). The novels are international thrillers, making 'Room 307' something of a change of pace.*

Room 307

Mischa Hiller

The bar-cum-restaurant was almost empty. Callum sat at a table alone, waiting for his chicken balti, a choice from a menu that included scampi and chips, a hamburger, lasagne, a club sandwich, and a vegetarian selection the specifics of which escaped him. He made to check the menu again but the young pimpled waiter had taken it away with him, as though Callum might appropriate it from the hotel as a souvenir of his unwanted stay there.

Across the room a group of young men were watching a large plasma screen. Some sporting event was taking place, rugby by the looks of it, and they would occasionally break out in cheers or derisory hoots. An elderly couple was eating at another table and two men in suits sat at the bar, ties loosened. It was too early for dinner, but Callum hated eating alone when it was busy. He always ate at the hotel he was staying at, rather than a restaurant in town, where he would feel even more self-conscious.

He sipped at his half pint of lager and studied the generic artwork on the walls. He had stayed in many of this chain's hotels and they all looked the same. Same faux-traditional pub decor in the restaurant, same anodyne and inoffensive prints on the walls, same bored staff in white and black, same tiny en-suite bathrooms with mouldy grouting round the shower end of the bath. They didn't even have a newspaper at reception he could hide behind, and he had left his petrol-station thriller in his room. He checked his mobile phone and thought he might ring Elizabeth, but it was best to save it for when he'd agreed to ring, or she'd think something was wrong and he'd have to explain why he was early. But then the phone rang and he could see from the display that it was her.

'I was just thinking about calling you,' he said.

'People always say that when you call them.'

'But this time it's true. Anyway I always ring you, you never ring me. Is everything okay?'

'Yes, I just wanted to catch you before you went out. The twins are in bed and I'm going to watch something on telly before turning in myself. I didn't want you to interrupt me. What's the hotel like?'

'The usual,' he said, wondering why she'd thought he would be going out; she knew for a fact that he wouldn't. 'It would be nice if the hotel was different each time, even if it was worse, just for the variety. What are you going to watch?'

'What?'

'On telly, what are you going to watch? I might watch it in my room, so we can compare notes.'

'It's not something you'd want to watch. It's an eighteenth-century drama thing with characters who have twenty-first-century sensibilities. Not your thing, trust me.'

'Okay.' He looked up to see the elderly couple make their way slowly out of the restaurant. The two men at the bar went to a table carrying drinks and menus.

'Anyway, I just wanted you to know that I miss you. I hate you being away so often.'

'So do I. Especially when the kids are so young.'

'Well, at least you mix with grown-ups and get a good night's sleep.'

She said this without rancour, as a statement of fact. He was about to tell her that he rarely slept when away from home, but it would sound like he was trying to make her feel better and she would berate him for not taking advantage of the fact that he could sleep uninterrupted.

'I love you. You know that, don't you?' She blurted this out and it sounded confessional, as if telling him she had pranged the car.

'I do now.'

'Seriously though. I know you're doing a job you hate and we'd only planned for one child, not two, not at the same time anyway.' She laughed and he snorted but this was not a discussion he wanted to have on a mobile phone in a hotel restaurant.

'We deal with circumstances as they happen, Elizabeth, that's what people do. Lamenting it isn't going to help either of us.'

She sighed. 'You're right, but sometimes one has to acknowledge that things haven't gone to plan so one can move on. It doesn't mean I'm lamenting, just acknowledging. Sometimes I worry that you've withdrawn somewhere else, or that you might find comfort somewhere else.'

'What do you mean?'

'Nothing, I'm just tired as usual, but I'm not sure we are dealing with circumstances, are we?' He was about to say something but heard her take a long breath. 'I know I'm not being the wife I was before we had the twins.'

'You don't need to worry about it. I'm not the same person I was before either.'

'No, I didn't say I wasn't the same person. I said I wasn't the same wife I used to be. I'm talking about, you know, marital expectations...'

'Yes, I know,' he said quickly. 'But it's inevitable with...' He lowered his voice and cupped his free hand over his mobile. 'Listen. I still love you. Even more in fact. We're just going through a difficult phase. A *different* phase. We'll get through it.'

It went quiet at the other end and Callum watched the two businessmen ordering from the waiter. The group watching the plasma screen cheered loudly.

'Elizabeth?'

'I'm here. Look. I wanted to say that I know you have certain... needs, being a man, and because I've not been able to...'

'This is not the time for this discussion, sweetheart, not on the phone.' He did, though, want to discuss it. She was right about the fact that they hadn't addressed it, even after six months. He wanted to know how they would move forward. That they could move forward.

'I suppose I'm trying to say that there's a difference between the physical aspect of things, and the emotional, and that for men—'

'Elizabeth. My food's arrived,' he lied.

'Yes, of course. So you're in the restaurant are you?' She sounded relieved at his interruption. 'Anyway, my TV programme is about to start.' He checked his watch. It was seventeen minutes past the hour; nothing would be starting at this time.

'Okay, just put your feet up and enjoy it.' He was going to suggest a glass of wine, but remembered she couldn't drink because she was still breastfeeding.

'Enjoy your evening,' she said.

'I will,' he said, his second lie in as many minutes.

He felt out of sorts after hanging up; it was a strange conversation for her to start on the phone when she hadn't brought it up before. There was something odd about it all. He wondered whether he should drive home that night. He studied the phone hoping that it might tell him what to do, but he had another meeting in the morning, and it was a three-hour trip so really it was out of the question. Perhaps he should call her when back in his room.

He took a drink of his beer and looked up to see a woman in a pinstripe trouser suit come into the restaurant. She was on a mobile phone and carrying a leather briefcase on a strap over her shoulder. The two businessmen stared at her like they'd never seen a woman before. She looked around, saw the group of young men and then hesitated, maybe looking for a table somewhere in a corner. She caught sight of Callum and he looked away. He realised to his embarrassment that she was hanging up the phone and heading towards him. He watched the two men follow her progress across the floor of the restaurant.

'Hi,' she said, in a throaty voice. 'I'm sorry to bother you but do you mind if I share your table?'

Callum, disconcerted, looked around at all the empty tables.

'Yes, I know, I could sit anywhere. But I'm a woman on my own and I'd rather not be chatted up by any of that lot. It's tiresome.' Looking at her, Callum knew she wasn't flattering herself; it was inevitable that one of the group would be egged on by the others to try his luck. Even a rejection would provide some entertainment. She pointed at his ring and smiled. 'I can see you're married, and you have a kind face.' The businessmen were looking towards him, probably wondering why she was standing at the table. He gestured to the seat opposite.

'Thanks, that's a relief. If you'd said no I'd have had to leave.' She undid the buttons on her jacket, sat down, and pushed her long brown hair over her shoulders with the back of her hands.

It drew Callum's gaze to her chest and he quickly looked away, scanning the room for the waiter. 'You don't have to talk to me if you don't want to, but it would make for an awkward dinner.'

'Sorry. I'm Callum.'

'I'm Susan.' They shook hands. Hers was soft with a gold band on her wedding finger. For some reason this reassured him. 'Have you ordered?' she asked.

'Yes, but nothing seems to be happening. Perhaps the kitchen is overwhelmed.'

She laughed. It sounded a little forced, but her brown eyes sparkled. She turned to look for the waiter and Callum caught himself looking at her slender neck and following the tendons down to a gold pendant at her throat: a small heart.

'So you're married too,' he said, after she'd caught the waiter's eye; not difficult with that smile. She turned to him and he noticed her left eye was slightly larger than the other.

'Yes, so I suppose we're both in the same boat.'

'How do you mean?'

'I mean we're safe with each other.'

'You mean if you were single and I was married, I am married, we'd be in trouble?'

'Or vice versa. This way we both have our marriages at stake.'

He didn't know what to say to that. Was she flirting with him? It seemed rather forward. The waiter came over with the menu and paid her careful attention, more than he'd paid Callum. She chose a chicken salad and glass of white wine. The waiter asked for her room number and she fished in her jacket pocket for her keycard and showed it to him. Callum could see that it started with a 3, which meant she was on the third floor. Callum was on the third floor, and for some reason this gave him a frisson. He asked the boy what had happened to his curry.

'I'm sorry about that, sir. I'll check with the kitchen. Would you like both meals to be brought out at the same time now that your wife is here?'

'Actually—'

'Yes, that's an excellent suggestion,' she said, touching the waiter's arm. The boy practically skipped off to the kitchen and she flashed her smile at Callum.

'So how often are you away from home?' she asked.

'Once a week at least, for one or two nights. You?'

'Three or four days a month, all over the place. And what is it that takes you away from your wife?'

'Two kids and a mortgage.'

'I meant *what* do you do, not why?'

'Do you know what, I'd rather not talk about it. Doing it is tedious enough.'

Her laugh this time was more relaxed and she tucked a stray bit of hair behind her ear. Callum wondered whether she wore it loose like that at work; it looked incongruous with the suit.

'Let's agree not to talk about our jobs, then,' she said.

Her white wine arrived. He felt a bit giddy sitting here with an attractive woman, then guiltily remembered Elizabeth at home. But it wasn't as if he had gone looking for company; she had come to his table and asked to join him. What was he to do, turn her down, make her sit on her own? Of anyone, Elizabeth would understand that.

'How old are your children?' she asked.

'One. They're both one. Twins, you see.'

'Twins. How exciting. Boys or girls?'

'One of each, actually.'

The food arrived and was put in front of them. Callum asked for more beer and Susan another glass of wine.

'At least this will go on expenses,' she said. 'What about you?'

'Yes, although there's a limit to what I can claim for dinner. The whole industry is tightening its belt.'

'Careful, you nearly started talking about your job.'

He laughed and she joined him. She raised her glass. 'Here's to expenses.'

He raised his glass and held her gaze as they drank, long enough for him to think, *what the hell am I doing?* But he worked hard, for Christ's sake, why shouldn't he have dinner with a woman, even flirt a little? The number of evenings he had spent alone in a hotel room watching crappy TV, not brave enough to pay for a porn film in case it was listed on the receipt that would go to his finance department. Instead he masturbated in the shower, picturing Elizabeth before the problems caused by the complications of childbirth. He couldn't decide whether clinging to an image of Elizabeth in the past was healthy, but then how healthy was it to be without sex for six months when you were married?

'It's difficult, isn't it, not having work to talk about,' Susan said. 'It doesn't leave much except the weather.'

'Sorry, I'm not very good at small talk.'

'I like that in a man,' she said, and cocked her head in a manner that he found sexy. 'You seem lost in thought.'

'Have you got children?' he asked.

'No,' she said, and he was stumped without a follow-up question. What could he ask: why don't you have children? It's not something you asked a woman. He watched her surreptitiously: she ate her salad with knife and fork, and left a crescent of maroon lipstick on the rim of her glass. She scraped a crumb from the corner of her mouth with a long nail.

'It must be hard work, having kids.' she said.

'Yes, but mainly for my wife. I can escape to work and middle-of-the-road hotels.'

'But you'd rather be at home. I can tell, you're a family man.'

Callum was a little annoyed at being described as a family man; it detracted from her flirting, even if it was accurate. But he was happy to accept the compliments of an attractive woman; what man wouldn't be?

'It's harder for her,' he said.

'It's hard for both of you. I'm sure she knows that it's difficult for you too.'

She was right, it was difficult for him, but perhaps not in the way she meant.

'Well, the positives outweigh the negatives. The twins, Emma and Joe, are wonderful, we can't imagine being without them. They've brought joy into our lives.' He felt a little silly adding that last thing but she nodded, putting her knife and fork together in the middle of her half-empty plate and picking up her glass.

'Have you got a picture?'

He did indeed have a picture, in his wallet, and he dutifully pulled it out and gave it to her. It showed Elizabeth on the sofa, holding one of the twins in each arm. She was smiling beatifically at the camera, which is why he had the photo with him.

'That's so lovely, your wife looks like an amazing woman,' Susan said, handing back the picture. Callum wasn't sure how she could tell that from the photo, but yes, he nodded in agreement. 'They must be hard work though, I bet. The twins, I mean.'

Why did she keep going on about how hard things were? 'Well, I prefer to think of it in terms of having to work for anything good. I mean good things don't just land in your lap, you have to earn them.'

She pursed her shapely lips. 'Sometimes good things can land in your lap. Although I agree that anything lasting probably needs a bit more work.' She smiled at him and it was devastating, that smile. Her eyes held his and he had to look down. Then, to cover his awkwardness he asked,

'Shall we have pudding or coffee?'

She stared at her half-empty glass of wine and Callum wondered whether she'd heard him. Then she looked up and her eyes had changed somehow, like she had switched into another mode. 'The food here is rubbish,' she said, and her voice had changed too. It was richer. 'And no doubt the coffee is too. I have some nice chocolates and decent whisky in my room. I always carry them with me when I travel.' She looked at him, cocking her head and smiling. He was sure she could hear his heart pounding across the table. She put her fingers around his wrist, as if taking his pulse. 'It's just for a drink, Callum, that's all.' The fingers told him otherwise. He managed to speak despite his dry mouth.

'I thought you were married,' he asked, sounding more accusatory than he meant to. She drew her fingers from his hand, stroking it in the process. It was a bolt of lightning to his crotch.

'I am. We both are. But sometimes there are fleeting opportunities that don't come again. Ships in the night and all that.'

The boy waiter came over and removed their plates, asking if they wanted to see the dessert menu. She declined for them both and he went off. The crowd of young men watching the TV started to rise as one, stretching and talking loudly. They moved to the bar area. Callum saw that more people were now eating, he hadn't noticed them come in. His mind was a blur and he didn't know what to say, never mind what to feel. Surely this didn't happen, this sort of thing, except in fantasies.

'Have you got a pen?' she asked.

He nodded, removing one from inside his jacket pocket and handing it to her. She took it and wrote her room number on her napkin. She gave him the pen and the napkin. She leant forward, close enough so that he if did the same their noses would touch. She spoke in a near whisper. 'I'm going to my room. I'm going to have a drink, run a bath, and relax. If you'd like to come and join me you're more than welcome. Something tells me you need it, Callum.' Her voice, or what she was saying, made his scalp tingle and his balls tighten.

'Is it that obvious?' he heard himself say, in a little boy's voice. Without removing her gaze from his she sat back and smiled only slightly, to show the seriousness of her intent. Then she got up and slung her briefcase over her shoulder, smoothing down her trousers and doing up her jacket. She gave him a long look before turning and walking to the door. He watched her all the way, and understood why the businessmen had been fixated. But this walk was just for him. At the door she glanced his way and smiled, then disappeared. The napkin was squashed in his tight sweaty palm. He couldn't quite believe what had just happened. Women didn't do this sort of thing, did they? Not married women, surely? Was he out of touch with modern-day female sexual mores? He told himself he was being sexist and unfurled the napkin: room 307.

He took the lift alone to the third floor and stepped onto the garish carpet. A sign opposite told him that left led to rooms 301 to 310, right to rooms 311 to 320. He stood looking at the sign as if it would offer some suggestion as to which way to go. The lift doors closed behind him, and to the left a door opened disclosing voices. He turned right and went to his door, fumbling with the keycard. Safely inside, he went to the bathroom and splashed cold water on his face, but avoided looking at his reflection. Perhaps he should ring Elizabeth. But he had already spoken to her and she would want to know why he was ringing again. She would detect the panic in his voice, hear the raging desire clouding his thoughts. But if he rang her it would put an end to it; he would not leave his room. If he didn't ring her he still had choices: go down the hall and have a drink, or stay in his room and watch

TV. He looked at his mobile phone for a long while, willing it to ring, then switched it off. He went back into the bathroom and peed, then examined himself in the mirror, combing his hair, then mussing it up. He took off his jacket, undid his shirt and washed and dried his armpits. Then he brushed his teeth. Taking a deep breath he left his room, walking down the hall, passing the lift until he stood outside room 307. He listened. There was no sound except for the pounding in his ears. He looked down the corridor towards his room. People were coming out of the lift. He knocked. A few seconds and the door opened.

She stood there in a short, belted silk robe that clung to her generous curves like shiny chocolate sauce running down a pudding. Candles lit the room behind her. The smell of bath oils came from the bathroom door along with the sound of running water.

'I'm glad you're here,' she said, turning back into the room. The door started to self-close and he realised he'd have to follow her in to avoid being locked out. When he got inside she turned and handed him a glass of Glenmorangie, which happened to be his favourite single malt. 'No ice, I'm afraid, it's not the Ritz. I'm running a bath for you,' she said, disappearing into the steam coming from the bathroom.

Something wasn't right about this situation. Something other than the dubious morality of him being here. He hadn't rung Elizabeth, she had rung him. She never rang him. What was it she had been trying to say? And then this sexy woman turns up to sit at his table, pays him compliments and invites him to her room. Her leather briefcase was on the side next to the bottle of Glenmorangie. Without thinking he lifted the flap and looked inside. There was nothing in there but a newspaper. Nothing. He understood what this was. This was a trap. A honey trap. A set-up to see if he would be unfaithful. He remembered a friend of Elizabeth telling them about it; you could hire a service to test your husband and see if he would succumb to temptation.

Then she was in front of him. The belt on her robe was undone and it was open an inch. Without the belt it hung straight down from her breasts, away from her stomach, seemingly held up by her nipples.

'I'm happily married,' he said, sounding like he had developed a sore throat.

She smiled. 'I know. So am I. This is just about tonight, Callum. It's nothing more than that.'

'Really?' he said, putting down the untouched whisky. 'Well, I don't cheat on my wife.' With that he turned on his heel, opened her door and reached his room in a near sprint. Safely inside he stood with his back against the closed door, laughing with relief. He thought about ringing Elizabeth but decided against it—let her sweat. Susan, if that was her name, would no doubt be reporting back at some point. Best to let Elizabeth think he hadn't cottoned on to her plan, that he had turned Susan down thinking her genuine. He would enjoy the moral high ground it gave him. He showered and went to bed, relishing both the vision of Susan in her robe and his self-restraint.

He forewent breakfast the next morning to avoid seeing Susan and went straight to his meeting. All day he couldn't wait to see Elizabeth. When he eventually got home that evening she was pleased to see him and he showed her extra affection, taking more time in looking after the twins, feeling smug as he did so. He looked for clues as to her relief at his behaviour, but she just looked tired and was grumpier than usual, more subdued. He took the twins out for a long walk to give her time to catch up on her sleep and thought about Susan in her robe, smiling as he relived the scene where he had rebuffed her advances.

After a few days his smugness receded and was replaced by anger at Elizabeth for setting him up; or was it because she'd not given him an opportunity to take credit? No doubt if he'd succumbed to Susan's silk-robed charms he'd be hearing all about it, but for doing the right thing he'd got nothing. But why should he? Now he wished that he had mentioned the incident to her so that she could congratulate him on his restraint, be grateful to him for his fidelity. But he'd left it too late for that. Instead he silently fumed, annoyed at her and her distrust in him. He was only human, after all; six months without sex was a long time. He went over her phone call on the evening in question once again; no doubt about it, she'd been an agent provocateur.

He had time to spare on the morning he was due to leave for his next trip, five days since he had avoided the trap. He drank coffee in the kitchen as Elizabeth snored in the bedroom, the twins asleep after their feed two hours ago. He himself slept in the spare room, at her insistence, and had done so for the last few months. She said, in her matter-of-fact manner, that there was no point both of them being sleep deprived, especially since he had to drive long distances. He was surprised when Elizabeth shuffled into the kitchen, bleary eyed and make-up free. He couldn't remember the last time she'd put makeup on. Couldn't make herself presentable but happy to get some tart to lure him into bed. But why? For a mad second he thought there might be someone else, but surely that was impossible? He needed to know, and it just escaped from his mouth, the question, surprising even him.

'How much did she cost?'

She stopped, then sat at the table, her head in her hands.

'How did you know?'

'Because you rang and said all that weird stuff. Because she fancied me. The last time anyone fancied me was...' He pointed at her. 'You.'

Elizabeth just sat there, looking shattered. He poured her some coffee and put it in front of her.

'So come on, what's the going rate for a service like that?'

She mumbled a figure.

'What was that?'

'Five hundred pounds, plus expenses.'

He whistled. 'Bloody hell, Elizabeth.' He shook his head.

'If it's any consolation, I got most of it back,' she said.

'You mean you only pay if the poor sap jumps in head first and gets humiliated by a refusal? Why do it, though? I don't understand? If you were so worried why didn't you just talk to me?'

'What do you mean?'

'I mean *communication*, Elizabeth. It's the bedrock of any relationship.'

'No, I mean what do you mean about a refusal?'

'Well surely it's the same amount of work whether the bloke falls for it or not.'

'Falls for it?'

'And isn't the woman putting herself at risk? What if I had gone into her room and then she'd turned me down after she was sure I wanted to go ahead? Some blokes might get ugly at that point.'

'I don't understand,' Elizabeth said, looking awake for the first time. 'Just what did you think she was up to?'

He sat down opposite her, his angry flow broken. 'Well, I assumed she was one of those services you hire to see if your partner is faithful or not. You know, they send some temptress to chat me up and report back on whether I was willing to sleep with her.'

Elizabeth snorted, an unhappy laugh cut short. She shook her head and looked at him pitifully.

'I don't understand,' he said.

She sighed. 'No, you obviously don't.' She studied him as if contemplating whether he could handle what she was about to say.

'Well?'

'She was an escort girl...woman. A high-class prostitute, if you will. I paid her to have sex with you without revealing her profession, as I thought you wouldn't go through with it if you knew what she was.'

Callum felt like he'd been slapped. He stared at Elizabeth who shook her head in disbelief, either at what she had done or the fact that he'd misunderstood her intention.

'You actually paid a prostitute to have sex with me?' he asked slowly.

'Yes. I thought you needed it,' she said, as if explaining why she'd bought him a new tie. Her hands, though, were clasped tightly as if in angry prayer. 'It made perfect sense to use a professional. It was better than you going off with some friend of ours or having an affair with someone at work, for God's sake. That would have been much worse. Sex for its own sake I can deal with. An affair is another matter entirely.'

'My God,' was all he could say. It all made sense: her phone call that evening, the woman's behaviour, that silk robe, his favourite whisky. A honey trap wouldn't have gone that far.

'She sent most of the money back, saying you hadn't gone through with it. I thought that was honest of her; after all, I wouldn't have known either way. I still had to pay her expenses.'

'But how, I mean where...?'

'Where did I find her? The Internet, of course,' she said. 'Then it was just a matter of an email and a phone call to explain what I wanted. She was very professional, very reassuring and had a sexy voice. I thought you'd like her.' Callum contemplated Elizabeth having a business-like conversation with an escort girl. He could almost hear her matter-of-fact tone as she discussed his particular needs.

'How did she know what I looked like?'

'Internet again. I directed her to your company's website. You're on there. I was on the phone to her when she was at the hotel, told her you were in the restaurant.' Of course, that's who she'd been talking to.

'She was a bloody good actor.'

'I'd hope so for that money. That's what you're paying for.'

'But five hundred quid, Elizabeth.'

'You could have spent the whole night with her for that.'

He started to laugh and so did she. They laughed until tears streamed down her face and his side hurt. He got up, went round and hugged her from behind as she sat in the chair. She smelled of baby shampoo.

'You know what's weird?' he said into her unbrushed hair.

'What?'

'The very fact that you would do this for me means that I could never go with anyone else. Never.'

'You say that now. But you're a man. You're led by your cock.'

'No, I'm not,' he said. He was going to offer the example of how he'd turned Susan down but realised that she now knew why he'd turned her down. Not because he didn't want to be unfaithful, but because he'd thought it was a trap.

'Anyway, I didn't do it just for you, I did it for both of us, for *all* of us. I thought that was clear.'

He took hold of her clasped hands and prised them apart to reveal hot and clammy palms. He rubbed them with his thumbs, not knowing what to say. He'd gone into room 307 before he'd had his supposed revelation about what was going on. The fact was, he didn't know if he'd have gone through with it. If he had, he would never have known it was Elizabeth who had arranged it. They would have both lived with their secret, except his secret wouldn't have been a secret. He wasn't sure he'd come out of this episode well. She, however, had come out of it selflessly.

One of the twins started crying. It was Emma, who set off Joe. Callum felt Elizabeth tense in his arms. He kissed the top of her head.

'I'll go,' he said.

'No, you've got to go to work and they'll need feeding anyway.' She got to her feet as he went to the door. He looked back at her.

'It'll be alright. We'll get through this,' he said.

She smiled sadly and looked away.

Somehow we've managed to wind up with three school stories in this book, each told from a different perspective. In 'Dress Code', we visit an American private school through the eyes of new teacher Joe Linus. Halimah Marcus is the managing editor of Electric Literature.

Dress Code

Halimah Marcus

The new dress code at Episcopal Academy, an all-girls private school on the Main Line, permitted students to forgo their uniforms once a week. Regulations were issued by mail in the final days of summer.

Linus knew there'd be problems as soon as he read the letter, which included a list of forbidden garments and areas of flesh.

A major infraction appeared on the very first casual Friday, which was regrettably Linus's fifth day teaching at the academy. The offending item was worn by Lauren Christopher, a blonde gamine Linus had already identified as highly influential among her peers. A sartorial epidemic took hold almost immediately. By the third Friday, Linus spotted them all across campus: seemingly harmless cotton with devilish touches of lace, coming in all colours, hoisted high and proud, framing the crests of young asses above hip-hugging trousers. Thongs. Thongs everywhere. The girls in Lauren Christopher's set, who numbered about eight, and all the girls who wanted to be, who numbered about a hundred, yanked their thongs just to the top of their low-riding pants so that when they sat down, bent over, crouched, or moved in any way, the forbidden T-strap was exposed.

The worst display was in the cafeteria, where cutouts in the backs of orange chairs framed these flagrant violations. Every Friday, Linus fled the cafeteria, head down, to eat lunch at his desk. He was only ten years older than some of the students and he tried to be practical about inappropriate thoughts: he had them; he let them go. He let them pass by without pausing to examine their origins.

It was during those weeks of cleavage Fridays, as Linus now called them, that he began to notice and appreciate Amanda Corb. Remarkably, on the first Friday, Amanda had shown up to class in full uniform. Linus assumed she simply forgot. But on the second Friday, when she appeared again in her blue pinstriped kilt, white button-up, and blue cardigan bearing the Episcopal Academy seal on the left breast, he knew she'd refused the whole thing. Linus found this choice equally rebellious and brave. More so because it offended two camps: it rejected the thinly sliced freedom the administration had so generously served her, and refused to compete with her cohort over purchases made during weekend trips to the mall.

And (he couldn't help but smile when he thought of it), there was the clever twist of irony, that she showed her non-conformism by wearing her uniform. He wanted to talk to her about it, only they didn't have that sort of relationship. She came into his class quietly, sat in the same seat by the south window, looked him in the eye while he spoke, and thoughtfully answered a question or two. Occasionally she even offered an unprompted insight. But, when the bell rang, she was the first out the door, never once stopping to ask a question.

Another week into the thong problem, Principal Field appeared at the teachers' conference for the junior class.

'A brief comment before you begin,' he said. 'My apologies for the intrusion.' Principal Field had the affected accent of an academic—vaguely British, dusty—combined with the slow speech of a man half asleep. Every Christmas he read the *The Polar Express*, a tradition rumoured to be so profoundly boring the school went on 'red alert,' which meant half the student body showed up stoned. 'I know you're all aware of the new Friday dress code,' he went on. 'In general it's going very well. The response has been very positive. But it has come to my attention that the violations have become exceedingly...distasteful. Please take the initiative to remind your students that exposed undergarments are not to be permitted on campus. I understand this conversation may be uncomfortable, but my secretary has prepared a cue sheet.' Principal Field passed a stack of photocopies to the teacher next to him. 'Stick to the talking points, and if you run into any trouble please do not waver too far from the approved script.' When everyone had a sheet, Principal Field paused a moment to let them read it over.

> [Student Name], have you read the dress code Principal Field's secretary prepared? Even so, I'd like to ask you to review it. Here's a copy if you don't have one. I'm aware the dress code does not state this explicitly, but we believe it is implicit in the dress code that exposed undergarments are forbidden. Do you understand, [Student Name]? You may consider this a warning, but further infractions against the dress code will result in detention. Thank you for understanding. Have a nice day, [Student Name]!

'Questions?' Several teachers raised their hands. Principal Field looked at his watch. 'No questions? If you change your mind, you know where to find me.'

Monday morning carried a new sense of relief for Linus, now that he knew four full days of wonderful conformity lay ahead. But Lauren Christopher was in his American Literature class and his homeroom, which meant, technically, that he was her advisor and responsible for reprimanding her about the thong. He had put off the conversation until, after nearly a week of inaction, Principal Field's secretary took the liberty of scheduling the dress code meeting on his behalf.

Over the past month, at roughly the same rate that he had grown to view Amanda Corb as a champion of his cause, a sympathetic compatriot, he had come to view Lauren Christopher as the enemy. On top of that, Lauren was a careless, uninterested student. The paper she wrote on *The Awakening* failed to reveal whether she'd bothered to read the book. Amanda, on the other had, wrote a sensitive essay about Edna Pontellier's suicide as a metaphorical return to the womb. He gave her an A- and Lauren a C+ and returned the papers on Monday, the week of his sartorial intervention with Lauren. He watched for their reactions. Lauren flipped to the grade and grimaced. Amanda's face gave away nothing, although she lingered on the last page, the one that contained his handwritten comments.

Mondays through Thursdays, Amanda was like any other student. All of them dressed the same in their matching uniforms, with only the small touches of earrings and make-up to differentiate them from one another. But even on a Thursday, Amanda carried the specialness she'd achieved the previous Friday; it lasted her all through the week.

Linus dismissed the class five minutes early and watched his students leave. When everyone else had gone from the room, Amanda Corb appeared at his desk.

'Oh, hi,' said Linus in a surprised and powerless way, like Amanda was someone's mother.

She held out her essay, folded to the last page. 'What does this say, Mr Linus?'

He leaned forward and read out of her hand. 'It says, "A convincing, well written argument, but what of it? Take it..."' he squinted, having trouble with his own handwriting, '"to the next level."'

'Okay,' Amanda said, and flipped through the pages, presumably looking for the next level. 'But what does that even mean?'

'May I see that?' Linus asked, wanting to give the impression he needed to be reminded of her essay. 'It means, so what? Your thesis is smart, but you need to move past just giving examples.'

'I worked very hard on this essay. It has eight paragraphs,' she said.

'I know. That's why you got an A. It's a great essay.'

'A-minus,' she corrected.

'No one's perfect,' Linus joked.

Amanda didn't smile.

'Listen.' He hesitated. 'If you want, you can rewrite the paper for the A.'

'I'm taking three AP classes,' she said.

'Right,' Linus said. 'You're the one who doesn't like the A-minus, so whatever you decide to do.' He knew the perfectionist in her would get him what he wanted.

Amanda didn't take long to give in. 'Fine,' she said, and they agreed to meet during lunch later that same week.

Amanda arrived promptly at the start of lunch period on Thursday as planned. Like many of the other girls she had taken to wearing an oversized shoulder bag in lieu of a backpack, and Linus thought the style looked better, more sophisticated, on her. In her hand she was carrying a paper grocery bag.

'I brought lunch,' she said, lifting the bag.

'You didn't have to do that,' said Linus.

Amanda shrugged. 'You're giving up your lunch period for me. It's the least I can do. Clear off your desk.'

Linus did as he was told, and Amanda began unpacking a series of plastic containers, paper plates, and plastic forks. The containers still bore their price stickers, all upwards of nine dollars a pound.

Linus struggled to bite his bruschetta. 'I've been wondering,' he managed, 'about your uniform.' An oily chunk of tomato dropped to his lap.

Despite all the food she'd brought, Amanda was eating almost nothing. 'What do you mean?' she said coyly, pulling her sweater forward and looking down at her chest. 'You know this is the first year I've gone up a size since eighth grade? I was starting to get worried.'

Linus blushed. 'I mean on Fridays. You don't do the casual thing.'

'Oh, that. I don't bother,' she said. 'It seems deluded to wear a uniform four days a week and then on the fifth day "express myself" or whatever. I do that other ways.'

Linus took the bait. 'What ways?'

'I play the violin, for one thing. See this callus on my chin?' She leaned over the desk and turned her head to one side. Sure enough, there was a small, hardened patch of skin slightly pinker than the rest of her face. 'I'm surprised you never noticed it before. It's hideous, I know, but I don't care. I just love to play.'

Linus found this impossibly charming. 'But you're not in the school orchestra.'

'Yeah. Well. Go figure.' She lifted a single noodle from the container of pasta salad. 'What about you? How do you "express yourself?"'

'I'm in a band with a couple guys from grad school. We try to practice once a week in a basement in West Philly, but sometimes it's more like once a month.' Linus suppressed the urge to cringe, knowing he'd included the basement detail in some ill-conceived effort to impress her.

'What do you play?' she asked.

'I drum.'

'You do not.'

'I do.'

'What kind of music?'

Linus had a prepared answer to this question, used mostly when talking to girls at bars. 'I guess it's punk rock with some prog influence.'

Amanda smiled. 'I thought punk was dead,' she said.

'Did you read that on a bumper sticker?' he teased.

Amanda gave Linus the laugh he wanted.

'Alright,' he said, 'Be serious. The paper.'

For the rest of the period, they spoke only about Amanda's argument. She'd come to the meeting well prepared, with an outline that included quotes for the revision. She even brought an article about psychoanalysis in literature that she planned to use as a secondary text. 'To give the whole thing a little more credibility,' she said.

Linus was tempted to open his grade book and just give her the A. But instead, he set a deadline and told her he'd see her in class.

The following afternoon, Lauren Christopher was scheduled for her sartorial intervention. All day Linus was nervous, hoping that Lauren would miraculously show up having already gotten the news, apologising for weeks of indecent exposure. Linus sat at his desk with Principal Field's script and the dress code placed squarely in front of him. Lauren wore a V-neck shirt that exposed both the cleft between her breasts and a slice of her midriff, and tight, low slung jeans. Three violations standing, four sitting.

'Lauren, hello. Please have a seat,' said Linus.

Lauren sat down. 'What's up, Mr. Linus?' she asked, and leaned forward, smashing her breasts up and together with her crossed arms.

It seemed to Linus that Lauren was acutely aware of her sexual power, how it was stronger than it ever would be again.

He glanced at the script in front of him. 'Lauren,' he began, having trouble looking at her, 'have you read the new Friday dress code recently?'

'No,' said Lauren.

'Even so, here's a copy.' Linus handed her the dress code.

Lauren made some sort of throat gurgle to indicate disgust.

'I know it's not explicitly stated in the memo, but we believe it's implicit in the dress code that exposed underwear is forbidden.' He managed a glance upward. 'Jeans and bare midriffs are also not permitted.'

'Okay...' Lauren said, and reached for her shoulder bag.

Linus kept on. 'You may consider this a warning,' he said. 'But further infractions will result in detention.'

By this point Lauren was standing. 'Is that all?' she asked. 'Can I go now?'

'Yes. That's all. Thank you, Lauren.' She left the room without addressing him further, her purple thong making a brief appearance as she lifted her bag and went for the door.

That following week, Linus's students were preparing their essays on *The Glass Menagerie*. In an effort to improve grades, rough drafts were due in class for peer editing. It was a rainy afternoon, and before class Linus stood at the window and looked out at the parking lot, where the yellow leaves of the ginkgo trees were turning to mush on the pavement. He thought of how he'd find them later, lodged in the treads of his dress shoes.

Then, coming from the building that housed the auditorium and the cafeteria, he spotted Lauren Christopher sharing her clear, bowl-shaped umbrella with Amanda Corb.

To Linus's knowledge the two were not friends, but there they were pressed up against each other, arms crossed at the elbow so that they each might wrap a white-knuckled fist around the cold rod of the handle. They were both barelegged in kilts and galoshes, walking briskly and breaking into periodic jogging steps, then laughing, and settling into a walk again. From what he'd observed of the social hierarchies at Episcopal Academy, a generous gesture like this one from the likes of Lauren Christopher was nothing less than an invitation to jump rank.

When they arrived shortly in his classroom, drenched despite the umbrella, Amanda didn't take her usual seat by the window but sat instead next to Lauren on the other side of the room.

When it came time to assign peer-editing partners, Linus paired Lauren with Amanda. It was typical for him to put a stronger writer with a weaker one, but the significant spread between Lauren and Amanda's abilities was bound to make Amanda feel like she was wasting her time.

But when they got down to business, Amanda and Lauren spoke in whispers intermixed with giggles, their elbows on top of the unread papers on their desks.

Linus had no choice but to cross the room and speak to them. 'Amanda. Can you tell me about Lauren's paper?'

'Sure,' she said, the gossip of a minute ago moving like a phantom through her voice. 'It's about the symbolism of the menagerie. About the fragility of the glass and how it reveals character.'

Linus picked up Lauren's paper and flipped though it, three pages that appeared to be triple spaced. 'There's nothing in here about the symbolism of glass,' he said after a pause. He picked up Amanda's paper, which was evident by the title alone that it was about what she had described: 'Breakaways and Breakage,' it was called, 'A Symbolic Reading of *The Glass Menagerie*.' Linus grimaced. Somewhere on campus, a teacher was telling the girls that two-line titles were better than one.

Linus looked at Amanda's paper long enough for her to know she was caught. It was a complete draft, eight pages single-spaced. Without saying anything further, he handed it back to her and returned to his desk.

After class, Amanda was the last in the line of students leaving the room. Linus pretended not to notice, and looked up only when she spoke his name.

'I'm sorry about today. I got distracted,' she said.

Linus didn't respond.

'It won't happen again,' she said. 'I promise.'

'Glad to hear it,' said Linus.

Still, she lingered.

'So you and Lauren, you're friends now?' he asked.

Linus imagined Lauren's impersonation of him, peevish and stammering, telling her to put away that thong. She'd probably acted the whole embarrassing scene out for her friends, which now included Amanda.

'Yes. Well, no.' Amanda looked ridiculously over her shoulder, as if someone might be standing there. 'Lauren thinks you have a crush on her.'

'That's ridiculous,' Linus said dismissively.

'I know.' Amanda became suddenly bashful and looked to the floor, as if she expected him to say something along the lines of *I like someone else.*

'Amanda, I can assure you that I don't have a crush on Lauren.' Relief surged through her face. 'Nor any other student,' he added for the record.

Her delighted expression didn't change. 'Glad to hear it,' she said, and was gone.

Before Linus went home for the day, he checked his faculty mailbox and found a memo waiting. At last, the administration had decided that the private meetings with students were not having the desired affect. As a means of damage control, Principal Field would devote the regular Friday assembly to the dress code. Linus was relieved. Already the emotional topography of the week was more than he could handle: between Lauren's disdain and Amanda's attention, he felt he had been up and down hills all day long. A school-wide assembly could put a lot of that to rest. Principal Field might even make them all wear their blessed uniforms once again.

That night, Linus drove to his band's practice space with a six-pack and played drums for two hours straight; no one but him, the results of the beer, and the syncopated smashing of his kit. At the end of it he felt better, and was able to go home and grade papers until he fell asleep with a stack of them on his stomach, body splayed out on the couch.

The assembly was nothing like Linus had hoped. Casual Friday would remain, at least until the end of the year and probably longer, provided the students began to respect the regulations. The school counsellor gave an elliptical presentation about self-esteem, followed by a suited woman who quoted from the school's handbook and admissions contract. Linus's eleventh grade American Literature class was directly after assembly, which ran over by twenty minutes. After all the students were in their seats, Linus looked around the room and realized he had no hope of gaining control of the class. The usual sight of identical paperbacks on every desk, which Linus always found comforting, was replaced by a slew of empty desktops and students shouting across the room without regard for his presence.

'If you want to talk about it, let's talk about it,' he said loudly enough to get their attention. 'Who wants to start? Tell me the problem with the dress code.'

'I just think it is unfair for teachers to tell us how to dress,' said Lauren Christopher. 'It's like telling us what to eat or something. It's fascist.'

Linus doubted Lauren had a working definition of fascism, but it seemed better to leave it that way for now. 'In every part of our society there are understandings about what people should wear. At work, people dress in appropriate attire. At the beach, people wear bathing suits,' he said, conscious of a younger version of himself, the teenage punk-rocker version, reacting to the resigned opinions of his adulthood. 'What's the difference between the school requiring you to wear uniforms four out of five days, and requiring you not to wear jeans on the fifth?' The question got no reaction. He tried again. 'What would you say if I came to school with an exposed midriff?'

'Ew,' Lauren said, 'That's totally different.'

Linus could tell he'd gotten to her, but still he had to exhale to dull the sting of her dismissal. He was right, but girls like Lauren were carefree. For winning an argument, carefree was better.

'I think it has to do with the intimate nature of being told what to do.' It was Amanda speaking now. She sat, legs crossed, in her uniform. 'The Friday rules are more personal than the ones for Monday through Thursday.'

'Thank you,' Lauren said.

Amanda continued. 'My parents can tell me not to wear something out of the house. I may not listen, but it makes sense that they can tell me,' she said. 'You can't. Because you don't know me.'

'You believe someone has to know you to tell you want to do?' Linus asked.

'Basically,' said Amanda. Several students around the room murmured agreement. 'And you can't know me unless I know you,' she said. The noise in the room grew louder, as it always did when someone took on the teacher. 'You know so much about us: who we date, where we live, our parents. But to us you're a mystery.'

'It's like when you see your teacher outside of school and it's totally weird,' Lauren said, and as soon as Lauren was behind it, the whole class joined in. A back-and-forth started up, students listing things their teachers knew about them that they didn't know about their teachers: who their friends were, what sports they played, their siblings. The list grew and grew.

Linus let them go on like that for a short while, trying to recall where exactly the rift in logic had occurred, how they'd gone from dress codes to a political need to know him.

'It's such a double standard,' Lauren declared over the mess.

Everyone in the room was talking except Amanda, who sat, proudly observing something she'd created, waters she'd churned up by hand.

It occurred to Linus that their sudden interest in getting to know him might mean he was one of the popular members of faculty, the one the students felt they could relate to. He was the youngest member of the English Department, and until now, his students hadn't seemed to notice.

'What do you want to know?' Linus asked, ostensibly to the room, but really to Amanda.

'Are you married?' someone called out.

'No.'

'Divorced?'

'No,' he said again. 'You only get one question each.' The two girls who'd called out groaned.

Over the course of the next fifteen minutes, the students learned where he went to college (Bard, on scholarship for poetry), where he grew up (Albany), what his parents did for a living (she's a librarian, he's a retired car battery salesman), and whether or not he went to prom (no).

Amanda sat and listened, saving her question for last. 'When in life were you the most afraid?' she asked.

Linus thought it over. He wanted to give her a good answer, an honest answer. He felt he owed her that. He considered saying, 'Right now,' as a joke, but that was ridiculous. It wasn't even funny. And, worse, it was a little true.

'Great question,' he said, and he meant it. Fear was not an easy emotion. He'd never been to war, never climbed a mountain, never put his life on the line in any real way, and so the fear he'd felt had always been disproportional to the situation. His fear was fear of other people. Fear of rejection. Fear of failure. Fear of himself.

'When I was in my mid-twenties,' he began, counting on them not to realize that was just a couple of years ago, 'I dated a woman who I later found out was into heroin.' The room was punishingly silent, and Linus saw that his last statement needed further explanation. 'If she was doing it while we were together, I had no idea. It's amazing what people can hide. But back then I liked girls who were a little more,' he paused to find the word, 'volatile. I thought it meant they were artists. Turns out, sometimes it just means they're addicts. After I found out about the heroin, we broke up. Not right away, though. I really thought I could help her. I would have stayed with her if she was serious about getting clean.'

Her name was Jenna, and he'd loved her severely; the only way she'd have it.

The truth was she'd ruined him long before he found out about the drugs: his love had made him impossibly needy, one ambivalent glance from her left him destitute.

'But once I was on to her secret, the lies really let loose. Talk about trying to tell someone what to do. Try telling someone to quit heroin.' Linus laughed once, and when it hit the walls of the room unreciprocated, it sounded to him like a dog's lone bark across an empty suburban neighborhood. 'Months after we broke up, she sent me an apology letter. I figured she was in NA, otherwise she wouldn't have sent it. "I can admit now that I'm a drug attic," she wrote. I'll never forget that. "I'm a drug attic." It was actually pretty apt. Anyway, after that, some guy she knew told me she was HIV positive. That was a moment when I really felt afraid. But also, I felt like an idiot; the possibility hadn't even occurred to me, even though I knew she was using needles. So I went and got tested and something about the test was inconclusive. They told me I had to wait six months for the results.'

As he spoke, he tried to remember the last time he told someone this story. It was probably Justin, his roommate during those six months at Penn when he'd convinced himself he would die of AIDS. He hadn't even told his band-mates. 'I was afraid for the entirety of those six months. I couldn't eat. I couldn't work. I lost a lot of weight and ended up taking a semester off from graduate school.'

The truth was he had never gone back, never graduated, which is how he ended up teaching at a private school in the first place, where they didn't require state certification. 'And then, at the end of six months, it turned out I was clean. Negative. Finally I called up my ex to tell her what I'd gone through, and it turned out she wasn't positive at all. It had just been a rumour, filtered through one of her junkie friends. And now she was nine months clean and I was the one with my ribs showing and circles under my eyes.'

Linus stopped, surprised by having come to the end of his story, like a staircase that he expected to have one final step. He realised, when he saw their stunned faces, that he hadn't looked at any one of them the entire time he spoke. His eyes were on Amanda now, since it had been her question, and he had a sneaking suspicion that this whole time he'd been staring at her knee. But she didn't say anything. Instead, she just looked freaked out. Really, that was the only way to describe the faces of all of his students: freaked out. They stared at him, let their eyes linger on more of him than usual, noticing, probably, the old band T-shirt peaking out of the top of his button-down, the Converse sneakers he'd opted to wear that day instead of dress shoes. Then they turned away from him and summarily changed the subject, talking amongst themselves for the few remaining minutes before the bell rang.

On Monday afternoon, Linus was called in to see Principal Field. The office was a serious place, all oak and Persian rugs, except for a framed poster that said, 'Your Principal is your Pal,' and featured a fun-loving cartoon pencil.

Principal Field offered Linus a seat and got straight to the point. 'I've received some complaints,' he said. 'First from Mrs Christopher, and now another parent.'

'Mrs Christopher?' asked Linus. Lauren had seemed fine since their meeting, after the initial embarrassment had past.

'I kept it from you because you were just doing what I asked,' said the Principal. 'I'm protective of my teachers. But even then, I questioned if I should speak to you. Her daughter was very upset.'

'But I used your script,' said Linus.

Principal Field removed his glasses, the way a therapist might, to get a better look. 'I've been hearing all weekend that you gave quite a speech on Friday. I hear you told your students your entire sexual history.'

'That's not—'

'You even talked about injecting narcotics. And the worst part of it, Mr Linus, is that Mrs Corb says the whole time you were talking, you were staring at Amanda's legs.'

Corb. The name felt like a skinned knee.

'It's all taken out of context,' said Linus.

The Principal wouldn't hear it. 'I'm afraid I can't discuss this with you any further. Not without HR present. I called you in today as a courtesy, since you're new to the academy and we both thought it would work out, in the beginning.'

Linus was only now putting it together. 'It's working out fine.'

'I'm sorry, Mr. Linus. I'm sure you're a very good teacher, but you're just not right for Episcopal Academy.'

'How do you mean?' asked Linus.

'Well, for one thing, you're wearing sandals.'

Linus looked down at his feet. It was true; he was wearing sandals. His toes were knobby and covered in hair. The dress shoes and socks he'd worn all day were in his bag, but the thought of explaining that to Principal Field, possibly requiring him to produce the shoes as proof, was more humiliating than the sight of his own primordial toes on the imported rug.

'HR will be in touch to discuss a severance package,' said Principal Field. He stood up and buttoned his coat.

Linus put out his hand. 'It's been a real waste of time,' he said when the Principal shook it.

From the Principal's office, Linus went to his car, walking briskly between the students' luxury vehicles to the faculty parking lot, which was full of decade-old station wagons. He got quickly inside his own station wagon, a wood-panelled clunker that had been his parents', and locked the door, not sure what would happen next. He didn't scream, as he thought he might, but he did punch the steering wheel, accidentally honking at a group of passing freshmen. They looked at him in that cruel way only teenagers can, and because he'd been fired, he gave them the finger.

In the outside pocket of his messenger bag, Linus kept the school directory. He withdrew the small navy blue booklet, turned to the Cs, and looked up Amanda Corb. She lived in the richest part of town on Old Gulph Road, known for its new money and ancient homes.

He tore out the page and pressed it into his breast pocket, telling himself he would never go there. Instead, he'd get drunk.

Linus had never before gotten drunk at a bar in these suburbs. He tried to think of some adequate dive nearby, and drove down Lancaster Avenue until he came upon the word BAR underscored by a pink arrow. Those unpretentious hot pink letters seemed to him, without exaggeration, like an oasis in the goddamn desert.

Inside, he ordered a whisky but upgraded it to a double when he saw the bottles were fixed with nozzles disallowing generous pours. He drank the double quickly, and looked around to see if there was someone to drink with. He imagined a guy like him, alone after a bad day, to whom he could tell the whole story. The guy would listen carefully, and then maybe he'd talk him out of going over to Amanda Corb's. 'Just don't do it, pal,' the guy would say. 'It would feel good, I can't deny that, but later you'll be sorry.' And because he'd called him pal, Linus would tell him about the poster in Principal Field's office and they'd order another round and have a good laugh at his expense.

But this was a sports bar with four TVs and there was no one like that here. Just a group of guys in white baseball caps, probably underage, eating hot wings in one of the booths, and an overweight couple taking turns choosing songs on the computerised jukebox. Linus ordered another drink and shot it. The whisky was cheap and made his toes curl against the rubber soles of his sandals. He asked the bartender for a third, along with beer to wash down all the whisky, and told himself to drink slowly and use the time to think.

He knew he should have some kind of plan for when he got to Amanda's, but really he wasn't interested in that. He just wanted to talk to her, maybe there was some explanation, something she could say to make him feel better. He'd foolishly believed that she understood him, all because of Fridays and her in that uniform. The truth was, he still believed she knew him better than any other student, and these days, that meant a lot. It meant too much.

When Linus quit the bar it was night. He found his car where he'd left it and drove, rather drunkenly, in the direction of Amanda's house. The residential roads of her neighborhood were illuminated only by the rare streetlight, and he made a couple of wrong turns before finding her street. He parked with two wheels in the rain gutter and headed up the hill towards the house. Gladwyne was a nice town the way Old Gulph was a nice road; nice, the way rich people say nice when they mean expensive. The yards were so big there were practically counties between neighbours, and the enormous stone houses were set back from the road, up winding black driveways that guided one's eye to disdainful front doors. Amanda's house was the biggest of all; a rectangle so large it probably had wings, like a giant bird.

Other than the outdoor garden lights, the house was dark. Low-lying and bright, they cast upwards on the face of the building, making it look like an open mouth. Linus supposed these lights were to keep away burglars, but really all they did was call attention to the bareness of the stone and the insincerity of the scale. Nevertheless, Linus rang the doorbell. He waited, but no one came. He rang it again. Still, no one. They were probably out at a play, or the movies. What did a family like the Corbs do on a Monday night, anyway?

By now, the Indian summer was gone and the bitter October evenings were beginning to make themselves known. No longer so warm from the whisky, Linus decided to take a lap around the house and see if it showed any signs of life. He set off counter clockwise, past the three-car garage, past the pool house, peeking in darkened windows but seeing only his own lopsided reflection. It seemed like he'd been walking forever, but still he was barely a quarter of the way around. He started to jog, his sandals flapping against his feet, toes slipping forward into the cold grass. He stopped and took off his shoes, held one in each hand, and continued jogging. The lawn was soft and well cared for, and there were no errant sticks or pebbles to injure his bare feet. To his right, he saw the lonely lines of a tennis court; ahead, a variety of rose bushes, no longer in bloom.

Arriving at the third corner of the house, he turned left, and his feet hit the smooth slate of patio, still warm from the day. The stone felt like a track underfoot, and recalling the hurdles he'd run in his own high school days, he leapt over a lounge chair, left leg forward, right leg tucked under, and then a wicker ottoman, and finally, a wrought iron end table. He rounded the last corner, into the home stretch and gave it everything he had. He pushed his chest forward through the front walkway as if it were the finish line, and collapsed, panting on the other side.

Fuck Amanda, he thought. Fuck Lauren, and fuck Jenna, too. 'Fuck, fuck, fuck,' he said aloud, and threw one sandal, and then the other, as hard as he could against the house. The first hit above the window and bounced back onto the lawn. The second he launched higher, and it settled out of sight, nestled in the eaves of the pitched roof above the front door.

Before he could hatch a plan to retrieve the sandal or decide to forget it and return to the car, he heard the sound of tires on the driveway. The car cruised easily up the new pavement, silver rims as still as if on a conveyer belt, and stopped just short of the garage. The headlights dimmed, and after a pause, Lauren Christopher emerged from the driver's seat.

A light turned on in the front of the car, and Linus could see Amanda sitting there, not wearing her uniform. She bent over to collect something at her feet, and so far had not spotted him. Lauren went around back and retrieved five or six shopping bags from the trunk. Then Amanda stepped out, carrying several more bags. They approached the ground where he lay, burdened by their purchases, teenagers returning from the kill.

Lauren saw him first. 'Oh my god,' she said. 'What the fuck.'

Amanda saw him too. 'Mr Linus? Where's your shoe?'

Linus stood up. 'It's on the roof,' he said.

'Do I need to call the police?' asked Lauren, holding her phone.

'No, no. It's fine,' he said. 'I was just in the neighbourhood. I need to talk to Amanda. Can you give us a minute?'

'I'm calling my mom,' said Lauren.

'Don't,' said Amanda. 'It'll be alright.' She put down her shopping bags and walked over to Linus.

He touched her elbow lightly and guided her a few more steps away from Lauren, who seemed afraid to move. 'Do you know I got fired?' he said, his hand still on her elbow.

She pulled her arm away. 'I'm sorry, I didn't.'

'It's your fault.'

'Look, it wasn't my idea to talk to Mr Field. I loved your story, that's why I told my mom about it.'

Linus didn't know whether or not to believe her.

'I thought it was really amazing how you opened up like that,' she said.

Still unsure if she was messing with him, he thought it better not to respond directly. 'What's the deal with you hanging out with Lauren, then?'

'I don't know. We're friends, I guess. We went shopping.'

'Shopping.'

'So what.'

'I thought you were better than that,' said Linus.

'What's that supposed to mean?'

'I thought you were the only one around here who wasn't superficial.' Linus looked over Amanda's shoulder at Lauren, who was craning her neck to hear.

'I'm not superficial. I just needed new clothes,' Amanda said.

Lauren took a couple steps toward them, and Amanda turned around and signaled her to wait.

'Listen, Amanda.' Linus put his hand back on her elbow. 'Could you do something for me? Could you play me the violin sometime? I'd really like that.'

Amanda looked at him strangely.

'And then, maybe if it went well, you could join our band.' The idea was so obvious, he was surprised he hadn't thought of it before. 'A lot of rock bands have violins in them these days. Of course you'd have to go electric.'

'I don't know, Mr. Linus. I'd have to think about it.'

'That's all right, Amanda. Go ahead and think about it. I know you have a lot on your plate.'

Again, Amanda pulled her arm away.

'My number's still in the directory, even though I'm fired,' he said.

'I better go,' said Amanda. 'Lauren's waiting.'

'Okay,' Linus said, but her back was already turned.

'What did he say?' Lauren asked. She practically yelled the question before Amanda had even reached her. Amanda picked up her bags and grabbed Lauren's hand, pulling her up the walkway to the front door.

The two girls went inside the house, laughing their heads off. The door shut behind them, and Linus was left alone, standing on the front lawn. Mercifully, their laughter could no longer be heard through the stone walls, and beyond his own breathing all he could hear was the expanse of the suburbs, thick and heavy like a blanket.

*Like many of our contributors (especially in the last volume), Colin
Corrigan is both a writer and a filmmaker. This is his second published
story, and he's apparently considering turning it into a short film.*

The Romantic

Colin Corrigan

Martin wakes up and looks at his watch, which is on his right
wrist, because he doesn't have a left wrist. He turns on his
bedside lamp, pushes back his blankets, climbs out of bed, and
pulls on tracksuit bottoms, an Aran sweater, his duffle coat,
and, with much heavy breathing, his wellington boots. He
opens the curtains: it's still dark outside, and all he can see
is himself and the room behind him, the lamp glowing in the
corner. His breath frosts against the cold glass and clouds his
reflection. He puts on his flat cap and wraps his scarf around
his neck; once, twice, three times. He picks up a folding chair,
goes out the back door, and walks through the empty yard, past
the disused stables, and on up to the top of the hill. Balancing
on one foot, he uses the other to hold the chair steady while
he forces it open, and sits down. The new day creeps over the
horizon, and colour is re-introduced to the world. He takes
his Moleskine notebook from his inside coat pocket, pulls the

lid off his blue fountain pen with his teeth, and writes the following words:

> When purple shadows turn to gold,
> When day is young and night is old,
> When dark is banished out of sight,
> I am glad to be alive!

Then he pens eight more such verses. Martin has been writing seriously for twenty-five years, ever since his left arm was amputated above the elbow after being crushed by an industrial printing press. He used the settlement cheque to buy his cottage, a half mile from Carraroe in Connemara, and he moved here from Dublin to concentrate on his art. He has written almost seventeen thousand poems, which he stores in his notebooks and types up on his laptop computer. He has sent those he is most proud of to various magazines and literary agents, but is yet to be published.

Martin likes to live in the present tense. He once wrote the following verse:

> Who can smell the future?
> Who can taste the past?
> The happiest man
> Makes every moment last!

...and though he has long since forgotten writing those lines, he is still of the same opinion today, as he stands for a final look at the sun, which has risen clear of the trees, kicks his chair closed and goes inside for his porridge with honey. He undresses, has a long, hot bath, and puts on clean clothes, then makes his bed and tidies the house. He wipes the dust from the bookshelves lined with many volumes of poetry as well as his own notebooks, hoovers the carpet, and sweeps the linoleum floor of the kitchen. Then, as it's not raining today, he takes the fifteen minute walk into Carraroe, where he has the cream of chicken soup and a ham and cheese sandwich for his lunch in the pub. In the shop, he buys fresh bread, eggs, and rashers, and then he walks back towards his house. When he is about half way home, he stops for a while to rest. He sits on the stone wall and watches the daffodils which are growing wild along the verge. Opening his notebook, he writes the following words:

> Yellow petals and thin green stalks,
> They dance beside me as I walk.
> 'Pick us!' sing the daffodils,
> 'And place us on your window sills!'

Martin has written almost eight hundred poems about daffodils, his favourite of all the flowers. When he arrives home, he makes a cup of tea and turns on his laptop computer. He types up what he has written so far today, and then selects an old notebook from his shelf, dated May, 1992, and begins adding these poems to his digital collection. He is particularly impressed by the lines:

> Your hair, the colour of the sun,
> Your eyes, they shine so bright,
> If I could hold you in my arms
> I would dream of heaven's light!

Although Martin has written poems about a lot of different things, his favourite subject is love. As he reads this poem again, for the first time in nineteen years, the face which inspired those words begins to emerge through the clouds of his memory. He can't picture her, exactly, but he can recall what it was like to be looked at by those eyes; he remembers a sensation of awe and excitement, and not a small amount of fear, and now he feels excited and afraid, as if she were there beside him in his kitchen. Details begin to float into position about her face, like strokes of water colour adding definition to her presence. She had worked behind the counter of the post office, and he had sometimes gone there to buy stamps even when he had no letter to send. He remembers wanting to post a letter to her with some of his best poems, so that she might know how he felt about her, but he didn't know her address. He moves his mouth, making a 'Kuh' sound, and he feels like he is about to think of her name. Then he remembers that he doesn't like to dwell on the past, and he slaps himself across the face. He finishes typing the rest of the poem, marks the page of the notebook with a strip of cardboard and returns it to the shelf, and shuts down his laptop computer.

On his way back towards the village for his dinner, Martin walks around by the ocean front. He sits on the stone wall and watches the sun go down over Gorumna Island. He leaves his notebook in his pocket, as he is worried that the wind might gust it right off his knee and into the Atlantic, but words like 'golden' and 'amber' glow in his mind. As he stands up to move on, he reaches around with his hand to the small of his back and pushes against the stiff vertebrae. He begins to wonder what age he is, but then he looks again at the sky, still streaked with a thousand reds and purples, slaps himself across the face, and climbs the small hill to the pub.

After cleaning the roast beef, mashed potatoes, turnip and carrot from his plate, Martin washes it all down with a pint of ale shandy. He feels tired then, after eating, and sits back in his seat to watch a nature programme on the bar's television. A young woman walks in through the door and orders a vodka and tonic.

She tells Paul the barman that she is from a place called Hartford in Connecticut, that her name is Aoife, and that she had never met anybody who could pronounce her name correctly until she came to Ireland. Her voice is so loud Martin finds it impossible not to listen. There are a lot of empty seats in the pub, but she sits down at the table right next to Martin's. She asks him if he lives in the village. She tells him that she is travelling alone because it's easier to meet people that way. He tells her that he lives alone because he is a poet. She moves over to sit at his table and says that she loves poetry, and she lists off all her favourite writers. Martin has never heard any of the names before, but he nods and smiles when each one is mentioned.

She finishes her drink, and he gets up to order another round. He carries her vodka and tonic to the table, then returns to the bar for his pint of ale shandy. She stares at him with her mouth open, and says, 'Oh my God! How did that happen?'

He stands next to the table holding his pint and doesn't say anything. She apologises and says that she had only just noticed that his arm is missing, and that he hides it very well.

'I can do everything with one arm that I used to be able to with two,' he says.

She shakes her head, her mouth open again, then says, 'That's great'.

'Except I have to scramble my eggs,' he says. 'I haven't had a boiled egg in twenty...'

He slaps himself across the face before he can finish the sentence. Aoife stares at him, her mouth open even wider than before. Then she laughs and says, 'You must be some kind of genius or something.'

He sits back down, and she tells him that the real reason she is travelling alone is because she broke up with her boyfriend a week before she left home, and by the time the story is over she has had two more vodka and tonics and he has almost finished his ale shandy. He goes to the bathroom, and when he gets back she has bought him another pint. She tells him about the places she's visited so far, and about her father. He watches the way she moves her hands in the air between them when she talks, like she is conducting the orchestra of her sentences. He notices how her blonde hair casts gentle shadows on her round cheeks and the slope of her chin, and how, when she laughs, her hair sways across her face like a curtain of light and shadow, and her eyes glint out at him like sapphires. He remembers again the line 'Your eyes, they shine so bright'. Then he hears her say his name, 'Martin!', and he looks around the bar. All the other customers have left, and Paul is lifting the last of the stools onto the tables.

Aoife tells Martin that she would prefer to continue drinking. Martin remembers the bottle of Powers Irish Whiskey in his kitchen, and they decide that she will join him for a nightcap. On the road back towards his cottage, Martin hurries to keep up with the speed of her steps and her sentences. He can hear his excitement pumping in his ears. He looks up at the three-quarter-full moon and the vast panorama of stars. He looks at Aoife as she bounces along next to him on the road, so full of energy and life! He tries to form lines of poetry in his mind, but the words—the moon! the stars!—fly about inside his mind and he can't hold them—her face! her eyes!—and fix them in place.

When they arrive home, he has to sit down for a moment, and Aoife finds the whiskey and two glasses in the kitchen and pours each of them a drink. She sits next to him on the couch—her perfume!—swallows two gulps of whiskey—her neck!—and stands up again. She walks around the room pointing out all the things she loves—such vitality! such radiance!—picking things up and putting them back in the wrong place—who cares! She begs him to read her one of his poems, and he goes to his bookshelf and selects the notebook dated May, 1992. She sits down on the couch and he stands before her. He takes a moment to compose himself. Then he reads to her the following lines:

Your hair, the colour of the sun,
Your eyes, they shine so bright,
If I could hold you in my arms
I would dream of heaven's light!

He looks down at her and notices that she is laughing, bent forward with her elbow on her knee, laughing and laughing. He doesn't understand what is so funny.

'I'm sorry,' she says, and she looks at him and hiccups. Then she is overcome by a fresh bout of giggles. 'It's just...you know...'
He looks at her, and then down at his notebook. He doesn't know.

'Do you not like the poem?'

'No! I mean, it's a lovely poem. It's just...' And then she's off again, her whole body shaking and rocking back and forward on the cushions. 'You know...' she says. 'If you could hold me in your armssz!' and she laughs so hard she rolls forward off the couch and onto the carpet.

Martin looks at the notebook in his hand, and then moves his gaze along his arm to his shoulder. Then he looks down to his left and he feels a sudden dart of pain where his other arm used to be. The pain shoots up through his stump and down his spine and back up into his brain, kicking him awake like a shot of adrenalin, and all at once he can smell the grease and the fumes. His foreman is shouting at him, because a roller has twisted sideways and caused the printing press to jam. It's hot and he's tired and sweaty. He grabs a wrench, and reaches in to open the nut that will release the roller. The wrench slips from his clammy grasp and falls onto a shelf below. His foreman is shouting at him. He reaches in to get the wrench, and beneath his weight he feels the press's motors whirr back into action. He tries to pull his arm clear but his elbow jars against his sleeve, and terror explodes in his mind as he sees his cuff caught in the splines of a turning cog, sees his hand's inexorable progress towards the whirling rollers. He hears the sound of crunching bone, the panicked shouts of his co-workers, and his own voice screaming out in agony and shock. He feels the cold solidity of the steel as he pushes and scrambles with his three free limbs. He tastes the steel in the blood squeezed from his tongue by his teeth. He feels himself being drawn into the machine, in and in and in.

The notebook falls on the floor. He blinks. Aoife looks up at him, holding her stomach. 'I'm sorry,' she is saying. 'I'm sorry.'

Ryan Shoemaker's story is our second look at school life. It's apparently inspired by the author's own experiences as a high school teacher, but I think he's used a fair amount of artistic licence here. At least, I hope so...

After All the Fun We Had

Ryan Shoemaker

Last year it was like these kids were just disappearing from our classrooms. Literally. You'd look and there'd be twelve empty seats when there'd only been nine a minute before. They'd sneak out the door, crawl through the windows if they had to. And God knows where they went. Sniffing glue in some back alley. Stealing beer from the Gas-n-Go. Those were usually good guesses.

And it's not as if their parents cared much. Our phone calls irritated them. They'd tell me to go you-know-what and then hang up.

And the few students who managed to stick around? About an hour of consciousness, until the Red Bull and amphetamines wore off, and then they'd be passed out and slobbering all over the desktops. Teachers complained. 'We're white noise,' they'd shout at me in staff meetings. 'We can't break through all the apathy.'

'Calm down,' I'd tell them. 'Calm down. Some decorum please.'

These crybabies knew as well as I did that we didn't have any leverage with these kids. Still, I threatened to take away the nacho bar in the cafeteria, to cancel Chicken Nugget Fridays if we didn't see a real change in attitude and a rise in attendance. I drafted an intricate code of conduct and posted one in each classroom. You know, how to sit in a chair, how to properly address a teacher, how to treat a textbook. Students cried oppression and then went elsewhere. We had too many empty seats. There wasn't enough money coming in from the State. We barely made payroll the last half of the year. We couldn't afford to lose another student.

The problem was these kids hated school. At best they tolerated it. They couldn't wait to get on the streets again. I'd hide behind the oleander in the parking lot and catch them crawling under the chain link. I'd lecture them on the value of education and quote statistics about unemployment rates for high school dropouts. They'd stare at me with those dreamy, molasses eyes. 'We're bored.' That's what they'd say. Bored! I was incredulous. It's not like they were headed down to Chase Field to catch the last innings of the Diamondback game. They wanted out of school so they could smoke a joint under a freeway overpass or tune into some stupid daytime talk show where people brawled and disputed paternity results.

Something had to change this year, or we wouldn't have a school. What the hell, I told the teachers, if all the oppression and the rules and Chicken Nugget Friday aren't working, then let's make it fun. Let's sink some money into it. Let's give these kids a reason to come to school.

We had our naysayers. I'll admit. We had some teachers who quit outright. But that was all right, because if school was going to be fun, it had to start with the teachers. We had to have some cool teachers.

First, I hired Mr Dingus. He taught carpentry. A hulk of a man. A jaw like a steel trap. Thighs like tree trunks. He oozed this heady bravado, had a palpable masculinity I thought our students needed. He'd be the father figure, the kind-hearted uncle, whatever, an alternative to the men in these kids' lives who'd never shown up for their birthday parties. He wore dark shades in the classroom. He spoke in grunts and clipped phrases. He could lift the back end of a Ford Fiesta. He was the cool teacher. That's what all his students said with a kind of puppy dog look on their faces: 'Mr Dingus is a cool teacher.'

And then there was Miss Beauchamp. She taught biology. Her resume came a week before school started. We were in a pinch. It was serendipitous. I mean, I knew it during our interview. I kept thinking as I looked at the chiselled contours of her tanned calves and the soft slope of her jaw, kept thinking that such a beautiful specimen was perfect to teach our bored students about homeostasis and cells and photosynthesis and reproduction. Maybe I'd never heard of her alma mater, some tiny liberal arts college in Manitoba. Maybe her grades weren't stellar. But she was a breath of fresh air, a stark contrast to Ms Leverkus, our biology teacher last year, a frail woman who wore ascots and hideous pastel polyester pants, so old and dried out, so boring and blanched of life, she eerily reminded me of the geriatric corpse I poked and prodded way back when in an undergraduate anatomy lab. No wonder our test scores in the hard sciences plummeted last year. These kids were scared of her. She smelled and looked like death. That gravelly smoker's voice, those spotted, veiny hands. She bore a striking resemblance to Cromwell's mummified head. Ugh! Anyway, she passed away suddenly in early August from some kind of blood clot or aneurysm, which really saved me the inconvenience and awkwardness of firing her.

So we had some cool teachers. Now I had to worry about the first day of school.

I envisioned a party, an event, a beginning of the year celebration these kids would talk about. Not some hot dogs and balloons. Something huge. A festival. A carnival. We had to get the word out, form an identity as a school where education is fun. I hired a place off Camelback called Got Party to handle the finer details. I told them to spare no expense.

So on the first day of school these kids trickled in, late as usual, eyes glazed over from a summer of excess and debauchery, stinking of reefer and cheap malt liquor. They stopped at the gates, gaping, taking in the blazing carousel in the back of the parking lot and the full mariachi band trilling near the school's entrance. They were dazed. Some, helplessly enchanted by the carousel's melody, reached into their pockets and pulled out greasy dollar bills and offered them to me. 'No need for that,' I whispered, leading them through the gates. 'Go. Eat. Have fun. This is only the beginning.'

We had a hundred students that first day, a hundred and fifty the next, and by the end of the week we'd maxed out our enrolment. I mean, we didn't have an empty seat. We were turning kids away. For the first time we had a waiting list. The money was pouring in, sixty dollars per student per day from the State.

Unfortunately, about a month into the first semester I got a phone call from Phillip Begay's mother. I guess he'd come home from school pretty upset. She wanted to know what happened. She thought Harris Mitchell had been pummelling her little boy again behind the Gas-n-Go. I wished it was that. No, Phillip told her that Miss Beauchamp, at the end of a lecture on the human reproductive anatomy in her all-boys biology class, had drawn a number of life-like figures on the chalk board in various sexual positions. I was shocked. Horrified, really. I mean, I was speechless. What could I say? I told Ms Begay we'd look into it immediately, that this was a serious matter, that any harmful contagion would be rooted out—my exact words.

Miss Beauchamp didn't deny it. She cried, she wrung her hands, she wiped at her streaming mascara. I volunteered my handkerchief. God, she was beautiful, like a woman in an old painting taken in sin. Anyway, she was frustrated. Students dozing off, smarting off. She wanted to connect with her students, have a laugh together, be the hip teacher. So when Vincent Lobato shot up his hand at the end of the lecture and asked how to do it, and everyone giggled, she got caught up in the moment. It was a lapse of judgment, a mistake, she told me. This was her first teaching job. You know how it is. That first year is tough. Lesson plans, classroom presence, classroom management, and let's face it, most of our students are rude and ungracious. So she drew a few figures on the board, nothing hardcore, really as a joke more than anything else, you know, to get a laugh from the kids. And that was that. There was a rumour that she'd mounted a desk while unbuttoning her blouse and told the class she'd make men of every last one of them before the end of the period. Totally false and ungrounded. Well, be that as it may, we had to let her go. A real shame. Really.

So we had that little problem with Miss Beauchamp, but our attendance was steady. Students were excited. They wanted to be at school. We had pizza parties, raffles and giveaways, a carnival with clowns and an inflatable castle, a concert on the basketball court by some local rapper who called himself Captain Boolicious.

Well, it got expensive. I won't deny that. Yes, we had to adjust our budget. Not everyone was happy, especially our cosmetology teacher, Ms Hardu. Last year I'd promised her a new classroom with recessed lighting and sinks and fancy chairs for cutting hair, some place she could open to the public so the girls could get their hours. She wanted a Zen-like feel to the room, a bubbling fountain, potted bamboo. It sounded expensive. I tried to reason with her, to show her our attendance, to speak to the greater good. She wouldn't have any of it. And then it hit me: have Dingus and his advanced carpentry class do it, you know, save a few bucks and let the kids build something bigger than a jewellery box.

'Cool,' Dingus said when I told him. He stared at me over his shades. A toothpick hung from his lower lip. 'Cool, cool.'

Well, they finished in mid December. Ms Hardu was ecstatic. She'd planned this big party, cookies and punch and a cheese platter, and even invited Sterling Couples and Rhonda Felski from the city council to give some prestige to the event, you know, make the kids feel they'd really accomplished something. It was wonderful, all of it, the cheese and the punch and the cookies, right up until the entire interior wall dividing the cosmetology classroom from the salon area came crashing down. You should have seen the chaos, the spilled drinks, plates of cheese and crackers flying through the air, the screaming as students clamoured under desks and into doorways. We thought it was an earthquake. Thank God no one was hurt.

Superintendent Flinders was irate, understandably. 'Somebody could've been killed,' he said. 'Somebody could've sued.' There was blame to assign, heads to roll. He wanted to know what happened. You know, why the wall fell.

What could I tell him? He knows as well as I do how these kids are. They get excited for about ten minutes when you let them hammer some nails or use the bandsaw, and then they're bored and want to destroy something.

It turns out some of the boys got hold of the nail gun and started firing it into the roof. I saw the damage myself, hundreds of little holes up there. Looked like an enormous constellation. And of course they pulled all the nails so they wouldn't get caught. And then we got all that rain. That's how the water got in. It was that second week of December. Three days of rain. Buckets and buckets of it. My laundry room leaked. My wife found black mould growing in our bedroom closet. Anyway, the water got in and saturated the wall.

The rain was understandable, but the real issue was the wall. Superintendent Flinders sent out this inspector to look at the broken mess, and this guy said it was a miracle the wall hadn't gone over sooner. He'd never seen anything like it, two-by-fours, two-by-twos, bailing wire and wood glue, a few nails here and there. In fact, he was surprised the wall had stood at all. Superintendent Flinders wanted to know why Dingus hadn't checked his students' work. He wanted to know if Dingus knew anything about carpentry. Dingus blamed his lazy students and the sub-par materials he'd been forced to use because of the limited budget. We questioned Dingus's TA, Marvin Sanders, who was tight-lipped about the whole thing and answered our questions with a lot of head scratching and incoherent mumblings, until we gave him a twenty-five dollar gift certificate to Applebee's. That really perked him up.

'And why hadn't Dingus checked his students' work?' we asked.

'Well, how could he if he wasn't in the classroom?' Marvin said.

And where had he been, we wanted to know. Marvin said Dingus and Miss Lorraine, the massage therapy teacher, had been doing some repairs in the utility closet behind the stage. Lots of repairs. We found a mattress in there, some personal lubricant and a container of whey protein. Nasty business. Unconscionable. Yes, we fired them. The students took it hard. As I said, Dingus was the cool teacher.

These kids circulated a petition to reinstate him, and then a petition calling for my resignation, because I'd fired the guy. They didn't get it. They live by a different code. Dingus was having sexual intercourse with Miss Lorraine in the utility closet and in their minds that elevated his status to that of a minor god. For a whole week they grumbled about the injustice of it. But then that Friday we had ice cream and pizza, you know, to smooth over some of that angst. They forgot all about Dingus when they saw the Domino's Pizza guy. Thank God these kids have short memories.

Well, we had a few setbacks, but the school year went on, better than expected, I should say. In January we brought in Randy the Reptile Man, and then there was Spirit Week, and then the petting zoo, and then the Valentine's Day dance at the Hyatt Regency. There was the Zapato Family Acrobats in early March and then Miss Boyle, our world literature teacher, complained that our students weren't getting enough culture and decided to bring in a troupe of Irish dancers, whom the students quickly booed off the stage. We made up for it the next week by bringing in some street dance team from Los Angeles called Epidemic Crisis. The kids loved them.

And of course every Friday during fifth and sixth period we watched movies and ate pizza. I'd bought a bunch of crap action movies from the discount bins at Walmart: *Quarter to Dead, Killer Piranhas 6, Pirates and Aliens.* But these kids weren't interested in action movies. All they ever wanted to watch was this saccharine Hallmark, made-for-TV movie I also pulled from the discount bins, thinking my wife might like it, some low budget piece of drivel about a dysfunctional family who befriend Bigfoot and learn to love each other again. These kids couldn't get enough of it. They'd watch it again and again, eyes riveted to the TV, wiping away the tears with grease-stained napkins. That's how these kids are. Just when you think you know them, they surprise you.

Anyway, all said we were having a great year. That I know. Kids were in class, maybe not doing much work, but they were there, they were attentive and courteous, and that counts for something. We finally had leverage. School was fun, a party, and nobody wanted to be left out for some bad behaviour. They wanted to be here. They were excited. I could see it in the way they twiddled their cotton-candy stained fingers and smacked their lips. They were always asking me what was next, who was coming to entertain them, when they would eat again. That's why we were so surprised about what happened at the end of April.

It was a Friday afternoon, all these kids gone for the weekend. We were having our staff meeting in the library, hashing out the final details for the school Cinquo de Mayo celebration. Ms Lipton was reporting on the Ferris wheel and big top we'd rented for the occasion, and then suddenly we heard a hundred voices out in the hallway. And then these kids started pouring into the library, shouting at us, their faces pinched and angry.

'We've barricaded the school,' they said. 'No one goes in or out until our demands are met.'

I stood there and faced them, and said not so gently: 'What do you have to complain about? We're planning a party for you. Aren't you having fun? Don't you look forward to coming to school? Last year. Remember last year?'

'We're tired of cotton candy and fire eaters,' they said. 'We want you to hug us. We want to be a family.'

'There are rules,' I said. 'There are laws. I can't hold you, I can't touch you. I could be fired. The State could shut us down.'

They pressed in on us. A raw, throaty vibration filled the room. I hadn't seen it before, but you know how these kids are: they had baseball bats, knives, and long pieces of chain looped around their hands.

'You'll be the father,' they said, pointing to me, and then they pointed to Ms Lipton, who looked ready to cry. 'And you'll be the mother. And you'll both sit in these chairs, and we'll be your children.'

So Ms Lipton and I sat there like stunned fish, staring at the wall, our hands resting on our thighs.

'No,' they told me. 'Put your arm around her. Rest your head on her shoulder. Yes, like that.' And then Alex Escobar came forward and taped a piece of poster board to the wall, a hand-drawn brick hearth with a blazing fire in it. And then he put up another poster, a New England winter scene, leafless maples covered with snow, a serpentine lane threading through dark woods to a quaint log cabin with glowing windows.

'We're frightened,' they said. 'Hold us. Tell us everything will be all right.'

They dimmed the lights and sat at our feet. Someone passed around steaming cups of spiced apple cider. They sipped pensively. They sang Christmas carols. I sat there clutching Ms Lipton's cold hand. Her eyes were pressed shut, her lips moved but no sound came out. If I so much as loosened my grip on her hand, I heard a chain rattle behind me. The hours passed. Above the school I heard the low whir of news helicopters, and from the parking lot the commanding baritone of a police officer shouting into a megaphone.

'This can't go on forever,' I told them. I was getting impatient. I had to use the bathroom.

'Shhhhh,' they said, their heads resting against our knees. 'Just a while longer. We'll be good, we promise. Shhhhhhh.'

Suddenly there was an enormous boom and then a blinding flash of light. The ceiling tiles collapsed above the doorway and twenty members of the city SWAT team dropped through the hole. The students ran for the door, screaming, vaulting over chairs and tables. The SWAT team was ready, strafing them with pepper spray and bean bags. They crumpled to the floor, squirming there like blinded newborns just pulled from the womb. I watched them with a stunned satisfaction as they rubbed their burning eyes and wept loudly. I took a step forward. I don't know why. I wanted to lecture them, say something about gratitude. But then three members of the SWAT team lifted me off the ground and whisked me away. My throat burned. I looked back at all those writhing bodies. These kids. So damn ungrateful.

Well, that's what happened, a quarter of these kids gone just like that, doing three to six months in Durango. I can't believe it. After all we'd done for them, after all the fun we'd had.

The school will survive. I think. Back to the basics: reading, writing, math. Nothing extracurricular, no pizza parties or carnivals. We'll probably lose another fifty students. Maybe seventy-five. I can already see their bored faces. Who knows, most of them'll probably be in Durango within a year anyways.

I've been to these kids' arraignments. I've seen them in court, lost and angry in those silly orange jumpsuits and black canvas slip-on deck shoes. I've heard what goes on in Durango, the bland food, those long, bored hours, lights that never turn off. God, I want to shake them, ask them if they're having fun in there. But you and I both know I can't touch them.

Andrew Jury has published several stories in genre anthologies and magazines, but is taking a step into the mainstream with this new story. Look out for more of his work in an upcoming issue of Postscripts *from PS Publishing.*

"Glenda"

Andrew Jury

Charlie's mother-in-law had never been one for keeping her big trap shut, especially when it came to her daughter.

'You know me,' she told Charlie one night. 'I speak my mind as I see it. Always have. No point pussyfooting around a thing like it's some delicate species of flower about to go extinct.'

That's fine, thought Charlie. Unless, of course, it's actually a delicate species of flower about to go extinct.

'I said—'

'I heard you, Glenda. I always hear you...'

'Then you agree.'

It wasn't a question, but Charlie nodded; though in his experience, speaking your mind as you saw it usually meant saying the first stupid thing that came into your head. Charlie had always thought he was more thoughtful, more considered in his views. He was considered in his view, for instance, that Glenda seemed to be spending an awful lot of time at his house these days. He was even considered in his view that Kathy, Glenda's daughter, was a bitch for upping sticks and shacking up with an over-groomed sales director in Bristol.

'...which is all I'm saying,' said Glenda now.

'Huh?'

'I just said, that's all I'm saying.'

Which meant she had just finished one of her rambling diatribes on the subject of her daughter, though he had no idea what the text of it was, having stopped listening five minutes ago. He grunted ambiguously and poured her another glass of wine. They were having a kind of barbecue—a *species* of barbecue, he thought, drunkenly—just the two of them, on Charlie's patio: if you could call pats of browned meat on hastily defrosted buns and wine that came out of a box a barbecue. Next door, Jim and Paula—'a couple of nubile twenty-somethings', Charlie had started to think of them, as though he were a much older man—had started up a game of badminton in their back garden to the accompaniment of a delicate Nick Drake track. All Charlie could see of the game was the shuttlecock occasionally arcing over the high fence that separated their two properties. Charlie had nothing against Jim and Paula other than the fact that they had raucous sex on Saturday nights in their bedroom adjoining Charlie's guest room; the one Glenda stayed in most weekends. Charlie had forewarned Glenda about Jim and Paula's proclivities that first night she stopped over. He'd even used the word "proclivities", as this was at a time when he was wholly, rather than just partly, uncomfortable around the subject of sex in the presence of his wife's mother.

'I see. So it's just Saturday that you hear them, right?'

Charlie nodded.

'So do you think they only do it once a week, or is it that they just keep quiet about it on a working night?'

'Why don't you go round and ask them?'

Now Glenda knocked back her third glass of wine and flexed a shapely foot out of her left sandal. Her nails were painted a fresh and deep crimson, Charlie noticed.

'Another?' he asked.

Glenda examined her empty glass. 'I shouldn't,' she said. 'If only because it's quite dreadful. Do you get it wholesale?'

'What do you expect? It's a box. It's a *box* of *wine*. If you want good wine, why don't you bring a bottle, like any normal guest?'

She laughed and he flipped over one of the pats of meat. It smelled disgusting; it smelled like what it was: death warmed up. Next door, Paula hit a backhanded winner—it sounded like a backhand shot—and Jim shouted, 'Your game!' There was laughter from Paula's side of the net, and Glenda said, 'Someone's getting lucky tonight' in a voice loud enough for most of Charlie's neighbours to hear.

Glenda had first come to the house on the Saturday after Kathy left him, and that same night that the two of them had gotten riotously drunk together for the first time. By the end of the night, Charlie had made it clear that there was no way she could drive home, and refused to even entertain the idea of a taxi (looking back, she had never once offered to book one). After that, Charlie never invited her again, and Glenda had never once asked to come over, but somehow she ended up sleeping in Charlie's guest room almost every Saturday night. She never brought an overnight bag, preferring instead to sleep in the clothes Kathy had been happy to leave behind, and which Charlie was less than happy to wash later in the week.

And now Kathy had been gone for over six months. Six months. That was a serious length of time. At first, Glenda had suggested, with no real conviction, that her departure was little more than a protest. More recently, however, she had come round to Charlie's view that it was probably a revolution, and when he closed his eyes at the end of the evening, there would be protestors standing in front of tanks, rioting in Grosvenor Square and dictators hanging by their heels in public parks.

'I'm partly to blame,' Glenda said now. 'I guess you should know that. Me and Kenneth, both. You never had a chance, Charlie.'

Charlie tipped his glass to her. 'Glenda, you have no idea how consoling those words are to me.'

'They should be, Charlie. They should be. Because she didn't get any of the good things from either one of us. Not a bloody thing. No, all Kathy got from the two of us was the brutal end of my candour and the flip side of his sexual fecklessness.'

'Sexual fecklessness,' said Charlie, and giggled. 'Now how about that? I never thought I'd hear those words coming out of your mouth. I'd like to hear you say it again at the end of the evening.' He put on his best amdram drunken voice. 'Seckswall fecklessssness...ness.'

He expected her to laugh, but she just narrowed her eyes.

'Charles,' she said. 'I'm trying to be serious for a moment.'

'Sorry, ma'am.'

'The way I see it, Kathy was doomed from the start. She was like one of those prototypes. An early experiment, like...like...' She twizzled her half-empty wine glass in the air, 'What's the name of that computer fella; ginger beard, glasses, geeky looking little bugger...'

'Clive Sinclair?'

'Yeah, she's like one of those silly little cars he designed.'

'You mean the C5?'

She nodded.

'You're comparing my ex-wife to a Sinclair C5?'

'In a manner of speaking, yes. Given enough time, he might've developed it into something less stupid, in the same way that Kenneth and I, given enough time...'

The rest of the metaphor eluded her. She stared blearily at her glass. Charlie wondered if he should refill it, then quickly did so. There were plenty of other boxes out back.

'Did I ever tell you how Kenneth died?' she asked him.

'Yes,' said Charlie.

'I did?'

'More than once.'

Glenda was referring not so much to her husband's death, but to the peculiar set of circumstances prior to her notification of it. Kenneth had wrapped his car around a streetlamp when Kathy was three years old. He was long dead by the time the emergency services got there, his torso almost cut in two. One of them found a purse in the backseat, and an imbecilic policeman, assuming it belonged to Kenneth's wife, had gone across town and explained to the woman (she was a trainee beauty therapist barely out of her teens with whom Kenneth had just terminated a very brief and unsatisfactory affair) how her husband had died, before making a second trip to Glenda's home an hour or so later.

'Only the lad's heart didn't seem to be in it that second time,' Glenda would always say. 'He was just going through the motions. Used up all his vast reserves of empathy and compassion on the little tramp, just like Kenneth.' And then the devastating denouement: 'Even in his death, I still managed to come second.'

In his less charitable moments, Charlie was of the opinion that the real pain this had caused Glenda at the time had, over the years, hardened into the material for a morbid, self-afflicted melodrama, in which Kenneth was the moustache-twirling villain and she the doomed heroine.

'Anyway, what did you mean, the "*flip side* of his sexual fecklessness"?' Charlie asked now.

'Huh?'

'The flip side, as you put it, would suggest that Kathy is sexually...what? Competent?'

'You know what I meant,' Glenda said now, irritably. 'And don't be so pedantic. God, you're such a nit-picker. It's not the sexiest quality in the world.'

He laughed, and a moment later her other foot slipped out of the sandal, and she began to massage her feet with the tips of her fingers. She was only twenty years old when she'd had Kathy, and Charlie was seven years older than her daughter. What did that mean? It meant that he was still a young man, and she was not an old woman...and as one friend had said, observing Charlie and Glenda together: 'You do the maths.'

'Perhaps you're right,' Charlie said now, just for something to say. 'Maybe I should hold myself more accountable.'

'Oh, God, listen to him,' she said, as though introducing a third party into the conversation. 'That's the wine in a box talking, or I hope it is. You're being ridiculous, Charlie. It doesn't matter a tuppence what you did or didn't do. Nothing would've ever been good enough for our Kathy.'

'What do you mean?'

'I mean she's become the kind of woman who could let down people for a living.'

It sounded like a line—a good line, but a line all the same—and for a second, Charlie thought about pursuing the matter. Then he shut his mouth quickly. Like all good double acts, they both knew when to speak and when to keep quiet. Across from him, Glenda reached for the spatula and turned the cow pats. Her blouse flapped open, and for a moment, Charlie caught the scent of her perfume over the stink of frying meat. He closed his eyes against the lowering sun, then opened them again. Something fluttered across his field of vision, a butterfly or daddy-long-legs. His hand came up instinctively to brush away whatever it was, and a moment later Jim's lovingly sculptured features appeared above the fence.

'Sorry, Chaz. Can we have our shuttlecock back?'

'Oh,' Charlie began. 'Depends...' He grinned, and the grin felt wolfish on his face.

'On what?' asked Jim.

'On...' Charlie had meant his 'Depends' to be the start of a joke, the precursor to a bit of neighbourly banter, but now the words failed him.

'On what, Chaz?'

The silence was there between them, a physical thing. Unless Charlie spoke soon, the whole situation would turn sour.

'It depends on...'

'...who's winning,' said Glenda, and as if responding to a cue, Paula's tanned and pretty face appeared alongside her husband's equally tanned and attractive one.

'Oh, I think I've got his number...Glenda, isn't it?'

'It is,' said Glenda. 'And you must be Paula...'

Charlie took this exchange as his cue to shuffle off to the corner of the patio where Jim's shuttlecock had landed. In the sudden rush of blood to his head, he realised that nobody other than Jim had ever called him Chaz. Charlie did not know Jim well enough for Jim to call him Chaz. Nobody knew him well enough to call him Chaz. He didn't call Jim Jimbo, did he? No, he did not. And why was that? Because Charlie wasn't a wanker, that's why.

God, he was drunk.

'Something smells good,' Paula was saying as Charlie ambled back.

'That'd be Charlie's baps,' said Glenda. 'Fancy a glass of wine? It's out of a box.'

'Not during a match!' they chimed together.

'Very wise,' said Glenda.

'The next game is the decider.'

'Winner takes all.'

'A fight to the death. Oh, thanks,' said Jim as Charlie reached up to hand him the shuttlecock. 'You folks enjoy your barbecue. Just shout out if we're making too much noise.'

This last line was delivered with a perfectly straight face, and a moment later the two perfect heads disappeared in unison.

'Well, what an absolutely delightful couple,' Glenda said, in a voice not quite loud enough for it to be heard over the fence.

'Behave yourself,' Charlie warned her.

'Well, that depends,' she said, and a moment later, they both laughed.

About a month after Kathy left him, a friend of Charlie's suggested he try counselling. This friend had himself been through a bitter and messy divorce, and could recommend the name of a remunerated Samaritan who had nurtured him through his own various crises; of confidence, of sexuality, or masculinity, take your pick really. Was Charlie interested? Charlie wasn't interested, he wasn't even half interested, but he went all the same, because his friend was the type of man who would cheerfully and robustly chide someone like Charlie into doing whatever he thought was best for him.

The counsellor was younger than Charlie had expected, and looked a little like Matthew Broderick, or more particularly, like Ferris Bueller on his day off. They were barely halfway through the session when Charlie realised he had less bitterness and fewer regrets about Kathy's disappearance than he had initially imagined. He still felt bruised and humiliated, yes, but even as he was saying these words, he recognised that there were no longer any real emotions attached to them. He talked about how he'd met her at an anti-globalisation rally in London; how both of them were there with partners who were far more politically committed, and who themselves might have hit it off, had they not hated everything about the other apart from their political views; he talked about the wedding, of course, and how he had felt more like a director on the set of a difficult movie than a groom, soothing egos, directing speeches, and preventing certain personalities from clashing with each other. He talked about his own mother, who, in comparison to Glenda, his mother-in-law, was old, old, old. Old fashioned. Old hat. Old dear. He explained how, after Kathy had left him, his mother-in-law ('"Glenda": that's how I always think of her, in inverted commas, not sure why'), had helped him to pick up the pieces left behind from his broken marriage—though in truth, there were only a few fragments, and the whole thing was barely worth patching back together. Besides, it takes two to tango, and I'm the only one prepared to dance, ha ha...am I talking too much, Ferris?

Halfway through the session, Ferris put down his pad and pen and told Charlie that he seemed to be talking more about Kathy's mother—

'"Glenda",' said Charlie.

Yes, Glenda, agreed Ferris (without the inverted commas), he seemed to be talking more about Glenda than Kathy herself. Were his feelings for his mother-in-law conflicted in any way?

Not knowing precisely what Ferris was talking about, Charlie just shrugged. Ferris, not to be denied, asked Charlie to sum up Glenda in one word. "Sexy" was the word that sprang instantly to mind (closely followed, admittedly, by "blabbermouth") but he couldn't say either of those words, so he just shrugged again. Ferris, clever boy, said they should turn the whole thing around. 'Give me some words that don't describe her, then.' And out they came, a torrent of words, and not one of them in inverted commas: tactful, subtle, shy, inconspicuous, reticent, demure, unprepossessing (where the hell did that one come from?), prudish, plain, boring, cold, homely, indifferent, old, unlikeable, unattractive. He expected Ferris to confirm his worst fears and offer him an apposite cure: drink more fluids, date a nineteen-year-old pole-dancer, take a course of strychnine. Instead, he made a quick note in his journal and told Charlie to come and see him at the same time next week. Which, of course, Charlie did not.

The next morning, Charlie was up early for his Sunday league fixture. His head was still throbbing from the previous night, and unless most of their opponents had also been up all night, he would be making an idiot of himself on the pitch. No matter. It was the last game of the season, and nothing other than pride was at stake. Glenda was still in bed, snoring lightly. He could hear her through the guest room door. He wondered if Jim and Paula had kept her awake the previous night. Probably not. They peaked loudly, but early, even on a Saturday night, and it was well after one in the morning when Charlie and Glenda had finally called it a night. He didn't recall much about the end of the evening. He'd rambled on about Kathy and her new boyfriend, and Glenda had talked about Kenneth and his infidelities, but he had no idea if either of these subjects had ever overlapped. That's how most of their Saturday evenings ended; the two of them simply talking about themselves in each other's company. When Charlie opened the patio doors to draw fresh air into his lungs, he saw four empty boxes of wine on the table and a barbecue cloaked in fat, grease and decaying meat. Charlie closed the doors quickly.

He wondered if Glenda would make an appearance at the match. He hoped so. He always enjoyed seeing his mother-in-law on the touchline, often late in the second half of a game. She would come wearing sunglasses, whatever the weather, and in clothes that were wholly inappropriate for a kick-about on an unploughed field. She stood alone on the touchline, away from the younger wives and girlfriends, who clustered near the halfway line, close enough to touch their men's kit bags and discarded bibs. Seeing Charlie in his shorts, she joked that he had nice legs, if a little white and hairy. The game itself seemed to pass her by; the only time she showed any real interest was when she tried to goad him into various acts of retribution against his opponents: 'When are you going to kick that dirty little bastard up the arse, Charlie?'

After the game, she sat in the pub with the rest of them and drank pints of lager and told funny, dirty stories about useless, unnamed men who were all Kenneth in one guise or another. The other players, some younger than Charlie, seemed to get a kick out of Glenda. Most of the women they knew over forty were either their mothers or their bosses, and so they were a little in awe of this sexy, older woman who teased and flattered them, who loved all the attention without ever once seeming to crave or require it. Even the older geezers who sat at the bar talking about local politics had noticed her. 'Reminds me of Sophia Loren in sexy middle age,' one of them confided to Charlie, his face going a little red, and Charlie said, yeah, I know what you mean, though in truth it was probably only the sunglasses.

As for Charlie, her presence in the bar—in his life—was increasingly problematic. She wasn't his girlfriend and she wasn't his relative; she wasn't even his mother-in-law any longer. What was she? His *common law mother-in-law*? Jesus. It was all so confusing. He'd never asked her to the football, in the same way he'd never actually asked her to stay over, but come she did, and on those occasions she wasn't there, his teammates were always disappointed, though none of them were ever as disappointed as Charlie.

That morning, Charlie spent most of the second half with one eye on the touchline, but Glenda never showed up, and when he returned to the house, turning down the usual post-match pint, his mother-in-law was gone. The bed in the guest room was neatly turned and there was only a thin glaze of steam on the bathroom mirror. A square of toilet paper blotted by a patch of blood or lipstick clung to the side of the toilet bowl. Charlie picked up a damp towel that had fallen off the rail and wrote the word "Glenda" in the condensation on the mirror, with the usual inverted commas. He could smell the fruity soaps and expensive shampoos Kathy had not taken with her, and which now only ever got used on a Sunday morning.

In the kitchen, Glenda had left half a glass of orange juice, most of a bowl of muesli, and a handwritten note on the kitchen countertop. She'd never written anything for him before. Her handwriting was small and compact, the letters packed tightly together, each sentence merging with the next like the carriages of an overcrowded train. She apologised for leaving so early, but Kathy had called Glenda on her mobile earlier that morning. She had some news that could be good for both Glenda and Charlie... but at this point, she couldn't say any more as Kathy had made her promise. Now Glenda was on her way to Bristol to see her daughter, and would call him later tonight or early tomorrow morning. It might not be a big deal, she ended the note, but then again...Either way, he should not get his hopes up too high.

She had underlined the word <u>too</u>.

Charlie read the note twice, once with very little feeling, and then again with no real feeling at all. He couldn't possibly imagine any news Kathy could have concerning Charlie that would be anything other than irrelevant, unless she'd won an obscene amount of money on the lottery and was going to share it with him out of guilt. He screwed up the note and stuffed it in his trouser pocket. Kathy and her either/or news meant nothing to him, but now he was angry with Glenda: about the note, about the manner of her departure, and about the mulch of messy cereal she'd left behind in the bowl. He went back upstairs to the guest room and sat on Glenda's bed, then read the note again. How could she get it so wrong? How could she have got him so wrong?

After a while, he went over to the window. The guest room, "Glenda's room", looked out over the back garden. From here, he could see that the patio was a mess, the lawn needed cutting and the flowers that had struggled up though the parched soil looked like dead soldiers on a conquered battlefield. Next door, Jim and Paula were stretched out on matching towels. Their badminton net was still up from last night. The rackets were laid carefully on the lawn, crossed lovingly at the handles. Charlie stared. He felt like he was watching a movie: *Charlie's Neighbours*. The perfect couple in their perfect world. Only if this was a movie, everything would eventually go wrong for them, and nothing would ever happen to Jim and Paula that they didn't want to happen.

A moment later, he opened the window and called down to them.

'Paula! Jimbo!'

They looked up at him, hands raised against the sun. He could feel the scrunched-up note in his pocket. Later tonight or early tomorrow, he would have to deal with it. For now, though, he had time on his hands.

'I'm having another barbecue,' he began. 'And I was wondering...'

'Get on Green', from American musician and playwright Jason Atkinson, is our third school story, drawing on the author's own experiences as a teacher in Washington DC. Jason's story 'Assassination Scene' appeared in Various Authors.

Get on Green

Jason Atkinson

'LunchPaks. Because a great lunch inspires great ideas.'

The TV is loud in the morning and it is the sign that my mommy gives to wake me up. My eyes open to see the boy eating his LunchPak as the other children watch him. They have normal school lunch. They are sad and wish that they had a LunchPak. They don't have one.

'Breakfast, Mommy?'

'You'll get something at school.'

'Okay.'

Mommy puts my shirt on. My pants. She looks at me.

'Put your shoes on, Tonya.'

I pull them over my feet. It's not easy.

'Can you tie them for me?' I say.

'No, baby, you can do that now, too. You learned how. Remember?'

I did learn how.

My mommy and I live near the big green park. They have big buildings over there like the Capitol and the White House, where Obamas live. I was dancing one day in a space over there in that park and I felt the sun come down and it made my arms warm.

'You did it! Good job tying your shoes, baby.'

I did it.

'Get your medical assistant degree now at Strayer University. Where dreams are made into...'

Mommy clicks the TV off.

College. Go to college. I have to go to college.

'Are you ready to go?' says Mommy.

'Can we take the stroller?'

'No. You're too old for that.'

'Please. I'm still tired.'

Mommy stares at me and I know she's going to say yes. It's good, because I'm four and my legs are tiny. My mommy's legs move her fast, too fast for me to keep up. She says I'm too grown for the stroller but I'm not. I'm just right for it.

I get in the stroller and shhhh. Then I fall asleep.

'Hello, everyone. I'm Michelle Obama, First Lady of the United States. Remember, always eat healthy!'

Obama. Obamas. Obama family. Michelle Obama gets on Disney and tells me I need to eat vegetables. She's the only one who gets on Disney, really. Her husband don't. Her kids don't. She's really the only one who comes and sees us.

'What are your favourite vegetables, Tonya?' says Michelle.

'Broccoli.'

'I love broccoli,' she says.

'Do you like carrots?'

'Yes. I love carrots.'

'I like carrots, too.'

'That's nice, Michelle. Would you like to have a carrot snack pack together?'

'Of course I would!'

Michelle takes out a snack pack and we open them up when Mommy shakes me awake.

'Wake up, Tonya. We're almost there.'

I get out of the stroller and walk a little. Walking helps me to wake up. Mommy talks to me to help me wake up.

'What colour are you going to be on today?' Mommy says.

'I'm going to get on green.'

'It's going to be an all green day, right?'

'It's a green day for me, Mommy.'

'Tell you what,' she says. 'If you are on green I'll get you a LunchPak.'

'Really?'

'Sure, baby.'

'The nuggets one?'

'Sure. Whichever one you want, baby.'

'I love my Mommy. I love my Mommy. '

She smiles at me.

'Here's your bookbag.'

Hannah Montana's face.

My bookbag has got Hannah Montana on it. One time I had a bookbag that had three princesses on it but now I have Hannah Montana. I like Hannah Montana. I like iCarly, too. I like everything on Disney.

I run to the school.

'Be careful with your beads.' Mommy calls out. 'Don't let them fall out!'

'Okay.'

Then I'm in school and I hug Miss Rain.

'Good morning, Tonya.'

I like the way Miss Rain talk. It sounds like the water when the ducks are floating on the water. It makes my brain feel like that. Ducks only float on the water when it is calm and good. Ducks don't float on bad water.

'Do you like my beads today, Miss Rain?'

Miss Rain smiles and touches a green bead.

'Yes. They're very colourful.'

I change my beads every two weeks. When Mommy does my beads I watch Disney or one of the shows that Mommy likes. It takes about an hour if she does them simple. If she wants to do them real good it takes about three hours. Today I have a lot of beads in my hair. I have a million beads in my hair today. If you're not careful, your beads will go flying. You have to be careful like me. I'm the most careful girl and I have never lost a bead. Never ever lost a single bead. I never will lose a bead.

'Do you have your homework today, Tonya?'

I stay quiet.

Miss Rain puts a frown on her face.

'Why not?'

'I forgot.'

'Don't you want to go to college?'

'Yes.'

'Then you have to do your homework.'

I nod.

'I'm going to get on green today, Miss Rain.'

'Good, Tonya.'

'I want to get on green and go to college,' I say.

Miss Rain always says that we have to go to college. That's what we have to do. We have to go to college. College. That's all we talk about, really. Smart people like Miss Rain go to college. Green people go to college. Not red people. Not yellow people. They go somewhere else. They go to the counsellor.

There are three colours at my school. Green is where they put your name when you do good. Red is where they put your name when you don't do good. Yellow is your warning. Yellow is where they put your name when you are not doing good and you might go down to red. Then they have a place that you start at the beginning of the day. That's the place where you aren't doing anything. You're not bad or good. You're just waiting to be put on a colour. I am there now. Miss Rain doesn't start changing colours until morning meeting.

'Let's all fold our hands and get in scholar positions,' Miss Rain says. 'Where are our hands?'

'Scholar.'

'Where are our hands?'

'Scholar.'

Miss Rain sees that I'm ready. I'm in scholar position.

'Good job, Tonya.'

She stares a long time at my table.

'Orange table please go to the carpet.'

That is my table so I get up and go to the carpet. I used to be on purple table but then they moved me. They moved me because I don't get along with the other girls at purple table. It's okay, because I like the orange table girls. They share food with me and we laugh and tell crazy stories about our lives.

When I stand up and go to the carpet I have to be careful. If I don't, my beads will go everywhere. Mommy says that after today my beads will be better and that I can run everywhere. But today I have to be careful. My beads need time to settle.

When beads fall out Da'Erica likes to pick them up. She puts them all in her cubbie.

'I got me twenty beads in my cubbie, Tonya,' she said to me one time.

'No you don't.' I said. But then she showed me and it was true.

'That's stealing beads.'

'No it ain't.'

Miss Rain starts morning meeting.

'Good morning, class,' she says. 'Today is Wednesday. Welcome to Morning Meeting. First, let's sing our college song. A one and a two and a one two three.'

I breathe in.

'We want to go to college. We want to go to college. We're gonna get the knowledge. We want to go to college. Gotta get on green to go. Gotta get on green to go.'

'Good singing, scholars. Can anybody tell me what day of the week it is?' says Miss Rain.

I am tired.

'Hey, Tonya,' says Hannah Montana.

'Hey!'

'Do you want to hang out with me?'

'Yes.'

'Let's go to LA and hang out.'

'What is LA?'

'LA is a fun place where all the singers are.'

'Cool.'

I was so excited because Hannah Montana wanted to hang out with me just like on my bookbag when she is smiling with friends. We went to many places together like the mountains and the city and the oceans and then Hannah Montana brought me to her house and we had a real talk about some stuff that she was going through in her life. Then Hannah, she said I could call her just Hannah, told me that she wanted me to go away. She became evil to me.

'Your hair is not as soft as mine,' she says.

'I'm sorry,' I say.

'Your skin does not shine as bright as mine,' she says.

'I'm sorry,' I say.

'Say it. Say that your skin is not bright and your hair is not soft.'

'My skin is not bright and my hair is not soft,' I say.

Then I open my eyes because Da'Erica is kicking me. She is kicking me because Miss Rain is staring at me. I fell asleep and Miss Rain doesn't like that.

'You have to get to bed on time, Tonya,' says Miss Rain. 'You missed all of Morning Meeting.'

'I'm sorry Miss Rain.'

'Orange table please get up from the carpet,' says Miss Rain.

Hannah Montana doesn't like me.

'Tonya? Are you going to get up?'

Hannah Montana doesn't like me.

'Tonya.'

Hannah Montana.

'Tonya! Orange table, please.'

'I'm purple table,' I say.

'No, Tonya. I moved you. Remember? You are orange table now.'

I'm just as good as the purple table girls. I'm pretty. I'm smart like them.

'Tonya. Get up and...'

Police car. Police car. The police car passes the school. The sound of the police car is loud and I have to hold my ears. Another. Another. Another. Angry sounds. They are angry sounds and one time I saw a man get put in the police car. We have to be quiet when the police car goes by.

'Tonya. Get up and go to the orange table or you're going to yellow.'

'No. No. No.'

I'm spinning. I'm spinning.

Miss Rain moves my name to yellow and I got up and ran to orange table.

'I don't want to be on yellow. Please.'

'No,' says Miss Rain. 'You have to make better choices.'

'Then can I get off yellow?'

'You have to make better choices first.'

'Okay.'

Reading. Spelling. Lunch.

Sometimes the lunch lady makes something good for us, but sometimes the food is not so good. I like Pizza. That's good. I also like LunchPaks and Plastic Juice Purple Blast flavour. Muminat and Da'Erica get both of those every day. Today Da'Erica got one that is a mini pizza and Muminat got one with the nuggets and the shaking powder.

'Eat something, Tonya,' says Lunch Lady.

I shake my head no.

'You don't like broccoli?'

'No.'

'What about these carrots? You don't like them?'

'No.'

'You have to eat something, Tonya. If you don't, I have to call your mom.'

'No.'

I don't care what Michelle Obama says. I can't do it. I'm not eating these DAMN vegetables. I said DAMN. I said it in my head so Miss Rain wouldn't know. Mommy would be mad at me for even thinking about DAMN. But I know all about DAMN. I say it in my head to keep it safe.

Playground. Helicopters. Obama.

'Who is it?'

'It is Obama,' says Miss Rain. 'He always flies with two helicopters.'

'Do you think Michelle Obama is with them?'

'Maybe.'

'What about Malia and Sasha?'

'They're at school. Just like you.'

Just like me.

I know all about the president. He's black. I'm black. We're both black together. I think he was on green more than me. He went to college. He got on green and went to college, that's what he did.

'Can I play now, Miss Rain?'

'Not yet. You are on yellow, remember? And you didn't eat your vegetables.'

'That means I have to wait five minutes?'

'That's right.'

'When is five minutes over?'

'Soon.'

I want to play. I watch the girls play clapping games. The all green girls. The good ones. They're all at purple table and every day they are good. Every day they go to green and they will go to college.

'Can I play now, Miss Rain?'

Miss Rain stares at me and I know she's going to say yes.

'Okay, Tonya. Go play.'

Miss Mary Mack Mack Mack. All dressed in Black Black Black. I love the clapping games and so I run up to the girls and push myself inside and throw my hands in the game.

'Tonya!'

'Tonya, we're playing right now. You gotta get back.'

'But I want to play.'

'No, Tonya.' She starts to talk like she is iCarly or Hannah Montana or something. Then she pushes me. I mean, I push her and then she pushes me. My beads go everywhere. All the colours rain on the playground. Green, yellow, red. The colours fall and roll away and Da'Erica gets on the ground and starts putting them in her pocket. She collects beads.

I go upside the green girl's head.

'Tonya hitting me!'

'You're DAMN right I'm hitting you.'

I start to pull on her hair and I rip some of it out. I'll take her hair out I'll take it out I'll take it out. Then I spit on my hand and I rub it in her face and put the dirt in her face. I'll kill her.

Miss Rain pulled me off.

'That's it, Tonya. You're going to the counsellor. And you are on red.'

Then she takes me upstairs and puts me in the room where I scream and I scream until my throat hurts. Once I am finished the lady comes in and talks to me. She is the lady that you talk to when you are in big trouble. We know each other. She is also good like Miss Rain.

'Do you want to do a puzzle?' she asks.

'No.'

She tries to look inside of my eyes. Past my eyes and inside of me. I don't let her.

'My beads fell out.'

'It's okay, Tonya. Your mommy will fix them.'

'She's going to be mad.'

'I'll tell her not to be mad at you.'

I don't say nothing.

'Why did you hit the girl?' she asks.

'They wouldn't let me play.'

'They were in the middle of a game. You need to wait your turn.'

'They were never going to let me play. They don't like me.'

'Why don't they like you?'

'Because I'm not good.'

'No, Tonya. You are good.'

'No.'

'You just have to wait your turn. Don't you want to get on green today?'

I nod. I want to get on green.

'My Mommy said she would get me a LunchPak if I was on green.'

'Ooh. That's nice. Do you like LunchPaks?'

'Yes.'

'What's your favourite?'

'I've never had one.'

'Well, maybe your Mommy wants you to eat right. LunchPaks are fun, but they aren't that good for you.'

'But I want to try it.'

'Okay. Well, I'm sure your Mommy will let you. But first you have to get on green, right?'

I nod.

'And why are you going to get on green?' she says.

'So I can go to college.'

'That's right, Tonya.'

'My Mommy's in college.'

'Oh. That's wonderful. What is she studying?'

'She is going to be in the hospital.'

'A nurse?'

'I don't know.'

'A doctor?'

'I don't know.'

'A medical assistant?'

'I don't know.'

'You should ask her what she is studying.'

'My Mommy says she hates college.'

The counsellor is surprised.

'Why would she say a thing like that?'

'She says that the college took all our money and tricked us. Now she can't get a job. She says college takes your money and they don't care about you.'

The counsellor lady stares at me and I don't know what she is going to say.

'No, Tonya. College is a good thing, Tonya.'

I nod.

'She says that she can never pay the money back to the college. She says she will always be poor.'

The counsellor looks at me. I can tell she is trying to think what to say.

'No, baby. That's not true. College is a good thing. I went to college. I loved college. College is a good thing. I want you to remember that.'

I nod.

'Say that with me, Tonya. "College is a good thing." Say it for me.'

'College is a good thing.'

'If you go to college you can be anything you want to be.'

I nod.

'What do you want to be?'

'I want to be Hannah Montana.'

'Do you mean that you want to be a singer?'

'Yes. I want to be a singer. And I want soft hair. And I want bright skin. I want to be beautiful.'

'What? No,' she says.

'No?' I say.

She touches my hair.

'You are beautiful already. Do you know that?'

I am beautiful.

'Touch my hair,' she says.

I touch it. The counsellor's hair is like mine. It's nice.

'My hair is beautiful,' she says. 'Do you think my hair is beautiful?'

'It is,' I say.

'Our hairs are beautiful,' she says.

'They are.'

Then she hugs me. She hugs me for a beautiful long time. And then she cries. She touches my face. She writes a special note on a special piece of paper. When I go back to class Miss Rain says I can go to green.

'But just this one time,' says Miss Rain. She smiles at me.

I walk over to the orange table and sit down. I touch my pencil to the paper and colour the picture.

I'm going to get on green. I'm going to get my LunchPak.

College is a good thing.

I am beautiful.

About the Contributors

Jason Atkinson is an American writer and musician, now living back in the US after three years in Italy. His story 'Assassination Scene' appeared in *Various Authors*, the first Fiction Desk anthology.

James Benmore was born in Kent and currently lives in South-East London. He studied literature at the Open University and has since completed an Mst in Creative Writing from Oxford University.

He is currently working on his first novel, *Dodger*, which follows the story of Jack Dawkins, better known as the Artful Dodger from Oliver Twist. It was awarded the AM Heath prize for fiction in 2010 (for best work of fiction by a graduating student of Kellogg College, Oxford.)

Colin Corrigan is a filmmaker and writer living in Dublin. He wrote the short films *Magic* (which he also directed) and *Dead*

Load. More recently, he has just completed the MA in Creative Writing at UCD, and got his first story 'Deep Fat' published in *The Stinging Fly* magazine.

'The Romantic' is his second story to be published.

Mischa Hiller was born in England in 1962 and grew up in London, Beirut and Dar es Salaam. He is the author of two novels, a screenplay, and several short stories. He lives with his family in Cambridge.

Andrew Jury was born and lives in Leicester, and works part-time for a health and safety company. He's been writing for over twenty years, and had stories appear in *Cemetery Dance*, *Lighthouse 5* and an anthology of speculative fiction, *Dark Doorways*. He also has a story due for publication in a forthcoming issue of *Postscripts*. Andrew's especially influenced by, and in awe of, many post-war US writers, most notably Tobias Wolff, Richard Ford and "the late, great John Cheever".

Charles Lambert has published two novels with Picador: *Little Monsters* and *Any Human Face*, as well as *The Scent of Cinnamon*, a collection of short stories with Salt. His story 'All I Want' appeared in *Various Authors*.

He lives in Fondi, a small town in Italy, halfway between Rome and Naples. Aside from the writing, he spends his days teaching English and working as a freelance editor.

Halimah Marcus is the managing editor of *Electric Literature*, a quarterly fiction anthology publishing in every format, digital and otherwise. Most recently, her fiction can be found in *Philadelphia Noir* and *The Fiddleback*. She is an MFA candidate in fiction at Brooklyn College and resides in Brooklyn, New York.

Jennifer Moore is a Cambridge University English graduate with an MRes on Witchcraft in Literature from the University of Strathclyde. Her short fiction and poetry have appeared in a number of publications on both sides of the Atlantic, including *The Guardian*, *Mslexia*, *The First Line* and *Short Fiction*. She was the winner of the Commonwealth Short Story Competition 2009. She lives in Devon with her husband, their two children and seven small fish.

Ryan Shoemaker is currently a PhD candidate in Creative Writing and Literature at the University of Southern California. His fiction has appeared or is forthcoming in the *The MacGuffin*, *Weber: The Contemporary West*, *Santa Monica Review*, and *Dialogue: A Journal of Mormon Thought*, where he won the 2008 Best in Fiction Award, as well as two New Voices Awards. Ryan lives in Burbank, California with his wife, Jennifer, and two children, Kieran and Haven.

For more information on the contributors
to this volume, please visit our website:

www.thefictiondesk.com/authors

Also from Charles Lambert:

Any Human Face

A dark and fast-paced literary thriller about love, sex, art and death.

When Andrew—a second-hand-book dealer—comes across a pile of photographs from police archives, he decides to exhibit them. But then the gallery is raided the day before the opening, and the photos seized with surprising violence. It soon becomes clear that someone, somewhere, wants to keep the images hidden.

Who? Why? And who—in a world where kidnap, subterfuge and even murder are the norm, and where no one is safe or above suspicion—can Andrew turn to for help?

'A sophisticated literary thriller set on the seamier fringe of Rome's gay scene, a magnet for the lonely and displaced located a long way off the tourist trail.' *The Guardian*

'Charles Lambert writes as if his life depends on it. He takes risks at every turn.' *Hannah Tinti*

'Charles Lambert is a seriously good writer.' Beryl Bainbridge

'A slow-burning, beautifully written crime story that brings to life the Rome that tourists don't see.' *Daily Telegraph*

A paperback from Picador.
New edition 4th November, 2011.
ISBN 978-0330512459

Also from Charles Lambert:

Little Monsters

"When I was thirteen, my father killed my mother..."

How do you recover from something like that? Carol never quite does. Sent to live with her aunt, who barely tolerates her presence, Carol is grief-stricken and desperate for love. Her Uncle Joey is the only one to notice her; years later, he's also the man with whom she builds a home and a life. But when Carol helps to rescue a young refugee from the sea, that life threatens to unravel, just as surely as it did when she was thirteen.

A paperback from Picador.
Out now.
ISBN 978-0330450379

The Scent of Cinnamon
& Other Stories

These stories deal with life, love, loneliness, delusion, misunderstanding, death. Their settings range from the colonial outback in the late nineteenth century to contemporary city life. The writing is comic, dry, satirical, vivid, magical, disturbing, poignant, spare. They describe the world as it is, and as it might be.

A paperback from Salt.
Out now.
ISBN 978-1844717392

Also from Mischa Hiller:

Sabra Zoo

It is the summer of 1982 and Beirut is under siege. Eighteen-year-old Ivan's parents have just been evacuated from the city with other members of the Palestine Liberation Organisation.

Ivan stays on, interpreting for international medical volunteers in Sabra refugee camp by day, getting stoned with them at night, and working undercover for the PLO. Hoping to get closer to Eli, a Norwegian physiotherapist, he helps her treat Youssef, a camp orphan disabled by a cluster bomb. An unexpected friendship develops between the three and things begin to look up...

But events take a nasty turn when the president-elect is assassinated. The Israeli army enters Beirut and surrounds the camp, with Eli and Youssef trapped inside. Are rumours of a massacre in the camp true? Will Ivan be able to salvage anything from the chaos?

'A stunning, defiant debut.' *The Guardian*

A paperback from Telegram.
Out now.
ISBN 978-1846590931

Subscribe

one year - four volumes
for just
£26.99

(wherever you are in the world).

Subscribing to our anthology series is the best way to support out publishing programme and keep yourself supplied with the best new short fiction from the UK and abroad. It costs just £26.99 for a year, so subcribers also save almost a third on the cover price.

We publish a new volume roughly every three months. Each one has its own title: *All These Little Worlds* is volume two. The next volume is due at the start of 2012.

Subscribe online:
www.thefictiondesk.com/subscribe

Also from Mischa Hiller:

Shake Off

London 1989: Michel is an undercover PLO operative hooked on
painkillers and posing as a student. He is tasked by mentor Abu-
Leila to find a venue for secret Palestinian-Israeli talks. But fellow
student Helen, forbidden fruit in this clandestine world, is proving
to be a distraction.

Michel is forced to go on the run when he takes possession of
a package smuggled out of the Occupied Territories and linked
to an assassination in Berlin—a package that both the Israelis and
the Palestinians are desperate to get hold of.

From the streets of London, Cambridge and Berlin, to the
remotest areas of Scotland, Michel must use his KGB training and
Helen's help to shake off his pursuers and stay one step ahead.

'Melancholy and dreamlike, Hiller's neat upending of conventions
movingly captures the realpolitik of a conflict perpetuated by the
shared interests of enemies.' *The Telegraph*

'In the best le Carre tradition...Hiller brings to his works not only
a craftsman's skill but also a compassion for his characters that
proves infectious.' *Haaretz*

A paperback from Telegram.
Out now.
ISBN 978-1846590887

Also from The Fiction Desk:

Various Authors

the first Fiction Desk anthology

These stories will take you from the shores of Lake Garda in Italy
to a hospital room in Utah, from a retirement home overlooking
the Solent to an unusual school in the wilds of Scotland. Meet
people like Daniel, a government employee looking for an escape;
and William, a most remarkable dog by anyone's standards.

Various Authors is the first volume in our new series of anthologies
dedicated to discovering and publishing the best new short fiction.

New stories by:

Charles Lambert	Matthew Licht
Lynsey May	Ben Lyle
Jon Wallace	Danny Rhodes
Patrick Whittaker	Harvey Marcus
Adrian Stumpp	Alex Cameron
Jason Atkinson	Ben Cheetham

Avilable to order from all good British bookshops,
or online at www.thefictiondesk.com.

£9.99

Out now.

ISBN 978-0956784308